CITY of SECRETS

Victoria Ying

Color assistant Undram Ankhbayar

VIKING

VIKING

An imprint of Penguin Random House LLC, New York

First published in the United States of America by Viking,
an imprint of Penguin Random House LLC, 2020

Visit us online at penguinrandomhouse.com

LIBRARY OF CONGRESS CATALOGING-IN-PUBLICATION DATA IS AVAILABLE
ISBN 9780593114483 (hardcover)
ISBN 9780593114490 (paperback)

Manufactured in China

10   9   8   7   6   5   4   3   2   1

THE GRAND CAPITAL CITY OF OSKARS

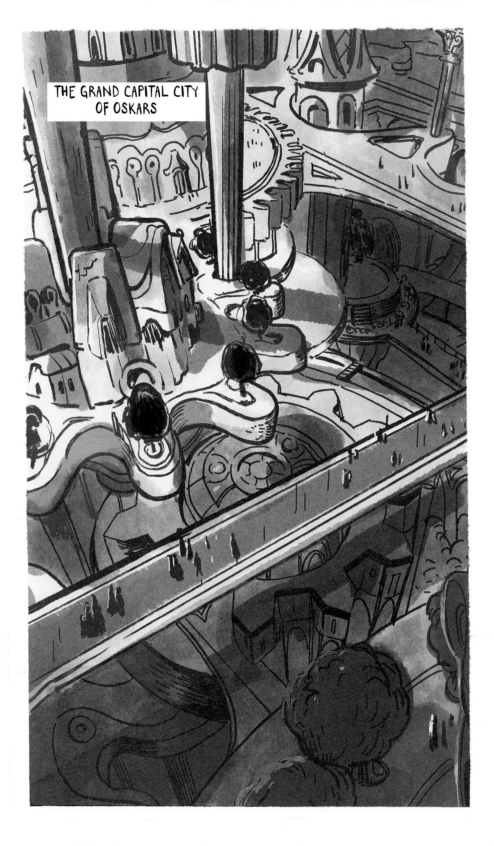

Hello, who may I connect you with? Ah yes, just one moment please.
THWACK
Lisa, sit up straight! No slacking today. Mr. Morgan will be here inspecting the Switchboard Operating Facility any minute!

Yes, Madame!

Madame is extra strict today. Are you alright, Lisa? You seem so tired.

I'll be okay, Anne. It's all of these rumors I've been overhearing . . .

I've heard them, too. War with Edmonda, our neighbors to the south.

Hey, did you bring an extra sandwich for Ever?

I did! It's only cucumber today though. We ran out of corned beef.
You two aren't feeding it again, are you?
He's not an "it," he's just a poor boy.
If you keep giving it food, you'll never encourage it to leave and live a truly productive life. Don't you care that you're making him more of a leech?

I'll tell her, I'll tell Madame you are feeding it.
If you do, I'll tell her about your little lunchtime visits from the baker's son!
W-what do you know about that?
BANG!
And this is the Switchboard Operating Facility, the beating heart of our capital city, Oskars. The girls and their work are the only things that keep our city's levels connected.

What a fine place you run, Madame Alexander. We are lucky to have you as headmistress of this amazing hub of communication.

Three floors and three basements, and you control it all!

Yes, I hear that the platforms and staircases all move, because this place used to be a theater. Is that true?

My, what a curious girl you have, Mr. Morgan. Should she not be better educated with a governess or at a school?

Ach, my Hannah spends every day with her governess. What's one morning out with her ol' pa? I want to show her around my new properties!

This place is amazing!

We do use the moving features of this building sometimes. For events, we often create a grand staircase.

It is a complicated facility, but I'm quite familiar with how everything works.

Must get to the lever before she tries to move the stairs!

Or else it will cause a chain reaction, and everyone will fall through the floor!

Level 1
Level 2
Level 3
Level 4
Level 5
Level 6

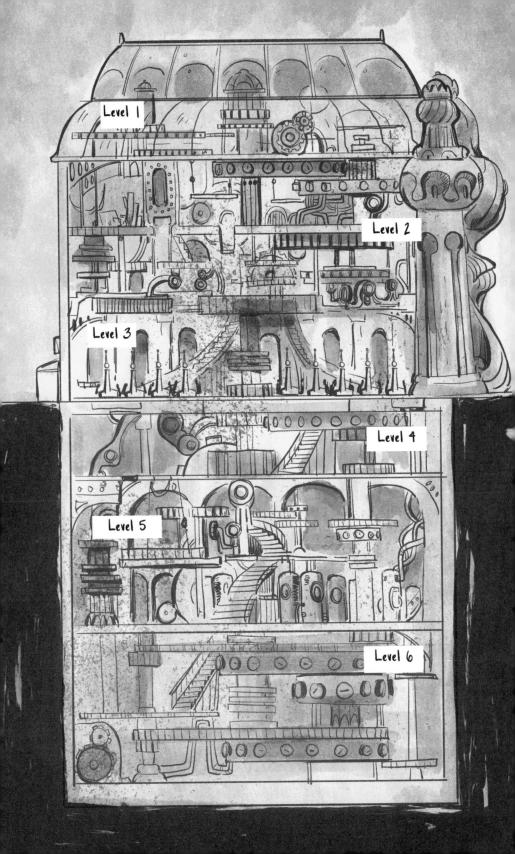

GRAB

If she pulls that lever, the platform they are standing on will drop! But if I can reach that control panel . . .

I can RAISE ANOTHER PLATFORM AND NOBODY WILL GET HURT!

WHOOSH

Oh no!

The lever also moved this catwalk!

WHOOSH

FWIP

CLAP

CLAP

CREAK

ERR

RK

GRAB

ROLL ROLL ROLL

WHUMP!!

KEEP OUT
KEEP OUT
KEEP
KEEP OU

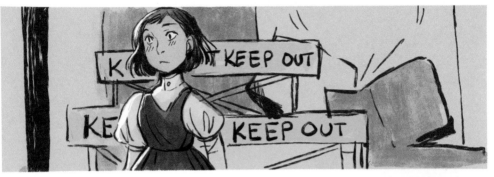

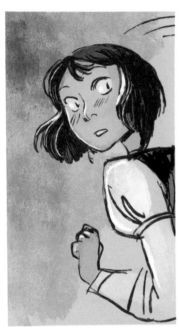

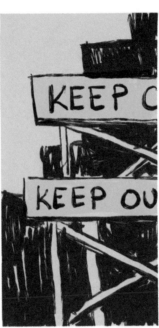

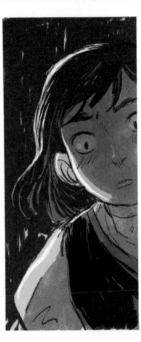

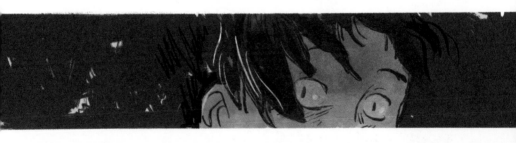

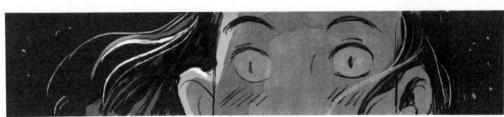

Hello?

Miss, you must be careful. This building is very old and some areas of it can be dangerous. Nobody knows how all of it actually works.

I thought I saw something in there . . . Something moved.

Hmmm . . . well . . . that's not quite a "something."

You heard a boy. He's an orphan named Ever Barnes. He lives here.

Lives? Here? In this place?
Lisa! Get back to work right this instant.
Yes, Madame!
Miss Hannah, you must be careful. These barriers are here for a reason.
I saw something.
Something?
Someone?
Well, someone.

Yes, a boy named Ever Barnes.

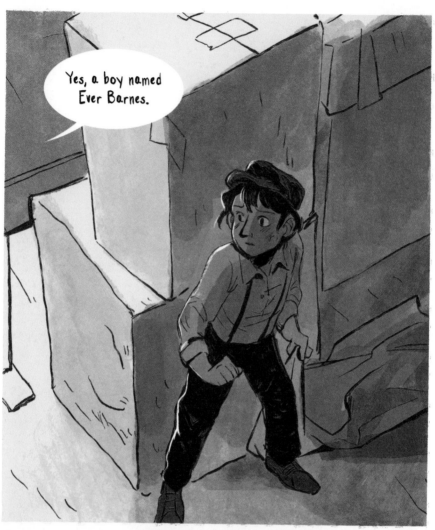

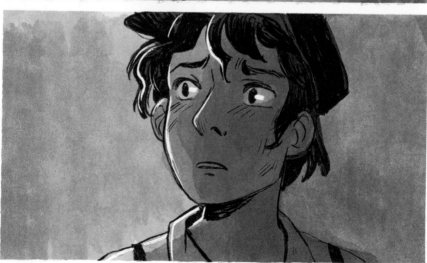

SOF
CLICK

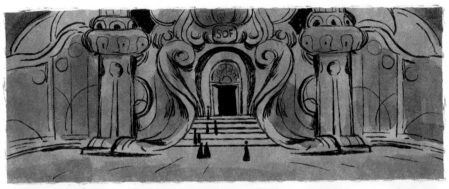

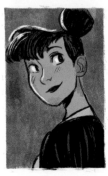

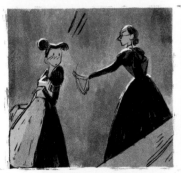

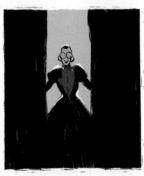

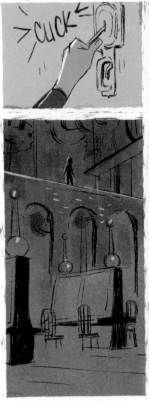

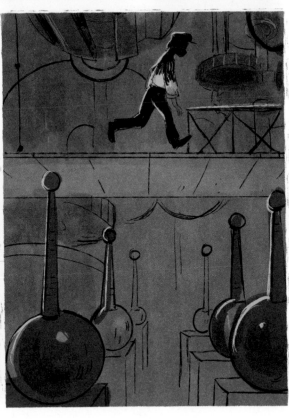

Now, Ever, I'm going to show you the reason why we stay here.

What is it, Father?

VRRRRRRR

Whoa! The whole building is moving!

We're not done yet!

ZIPPPP

Watch closely now, Ever. You will need to remember. This secret has been entrusted to our family for generations.
A secret that will save our beloved Oskars.
Why would we need to save our city?
Well, we don't know yet. But if something were to happen . . .
This is it.
A secret room?
No, Ever, it's a SECRET SAFE

What's inside of it?
The safe holds the secret. We've been lucky because we haven't had to open it, so I can't say for sure. All I know is that we must guard it and make sure it stays hidden.
Why do we need to guard it?
We do this for the good of everyone in our city. So they can be safe.
What's the secret? What are we guarding? What's keeping everyone safe?
Do you trust me?

Yes.

Good. I trust you too, Ever, as I trusted my father when he told me what I'm about to tell you: You know all you need to know for now.

There is more to this secret, but it's something you will learn in time, when you're a little older.

Simply protecting this very important secret and keeping this safe hidden is all you need to know now. Trust me, Ever, sometimes too much information is dangerous.

So, it's you and me protecting this secret together. Okay?

Okay.

Level 3

Madame, this car is going DOWN. The UP train is on the opposite track.

SHRUG

ding ding

ding

Level Four!

Love potions! Curses! Charms! Rarities and oddities from Level Six!

A love potion! That's just what I need for Mr. Laffoon! You really CAN find anything in this market!

You don't need that! He's almost ready to propose! Besides, you know that those things aren't real.

It couldn't hurt!

Ah, you ladies must be from Level One!

No worries, ladies, I know well how to keep a secret in a city like Oskars. Speaking of secrets...

Those silly girls. Everyone knows that magic isn't real.

Ah! Madame—

DON'T speak my name. Where do you think we are?

I think if you are here, then we both already know exactly where we are.

Though, I do forget sometimes how the upper levels feel about here . . . about us. But you all still like our wares. Come inside then.

So, you say you have a pest running around in your place of employment?

I'm far from a simple employee, Cooke. I am the manager of the Switchboard Operating Facility, the communication center of the entire capital.

And I would very much like to be rid of this problem.

The switchboard, eh? That's one interesting building . . . An ancient building, some would say.

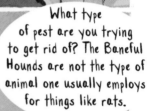

What type of pest are you trying to get rid of? The Baneful Hounds are not the type of animal one usually employs for things like rats.

A boy.

A boy?

Children can be vermin. Ugly, dirty little things.
Where are they?
Right through here.

>CLICK<

The Baneful Hounds.

C-c-can they hunt?

You use this whistle to control them. There is only one in existence. These dogs live up to their . . . reputation.

Can they kill?

FWEE!

ARF

BARK

SNARL

SCRATCH

ARF

ARF ARF! SNARK
ARF AR
ARF! BARK! BARK! BARK!
Good.

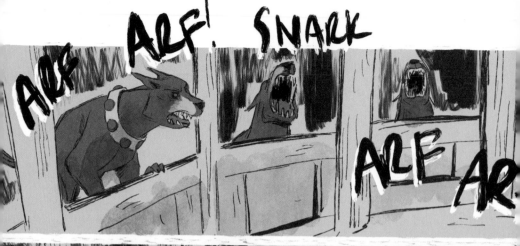

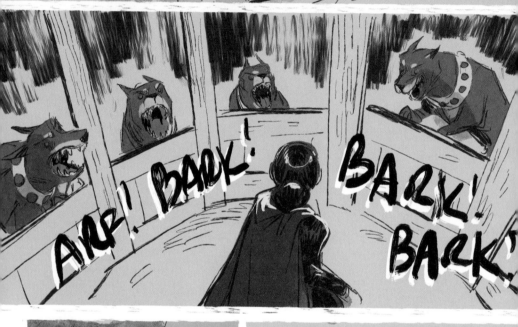

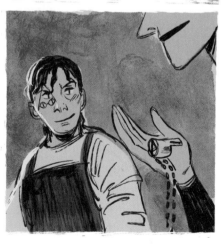

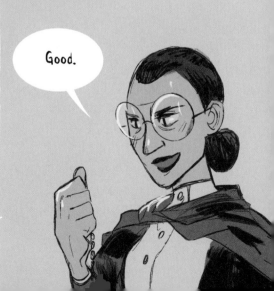

Miss Hannah! I didn't know you were coming. I would have had Ness saddled for you.

That's alright, Greene. I'm actually looking for Jimmy.

He isn't around today. Why don't you give Ness a ride? Besides, little miss, your parents are going to wonder why your riding hasn't improved if you keep lying to them about where you're going.

I'm getting better at lots of other things, though.

Oh? Like what?

I can climb the big tree by the mausoleum in three minutes flat! That's faster than Jimmy or John!

Miss Hannah, those stable boys could lose their jobs if you keep distracting them from their work.

It's been hard 'round here, miss. I will only need one more horse groom in the next year.

...and the other boys will have to go find work somewhere else when they get too old to be stable boys.

Besides, you're getting older yourself. You shouldn't be out roughhousing the way you were when you were just a child.

You have lady things to do, miss.

Why does everyone keep saying that?

Because it's true.

NUZZ NUZZLE

Ness misses you, too. Why don't you go to the kitchen and see if Mrs. Byrd has an apple for her while I get her saddled for you.

Alright.

Let me help you!
Oh, Jimmy! It's you!
Miss!
I was looking for you earlier! What are you doing out here?

Well, miss, Mr. Greene said he will only need one more groom next year so I need to be useful if I want to keep a position here.
I'm sorry—
No, I'm sorry. I didn't mean to cause trouble.
I—I have to get these to the kitchen . . .
Okay.

PLIP
PLIP
PLIP
PLIP
PLIP
Four years ago
PLIP
PLIP
PLIP
Father . . .
PLIP
PLIP
PLIP

SHINK

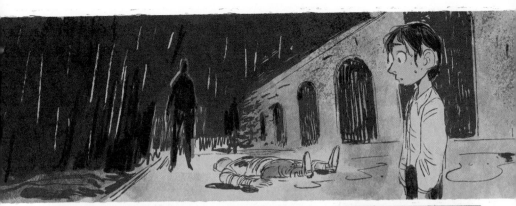

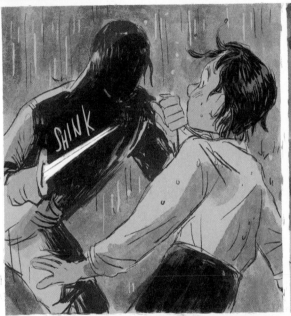

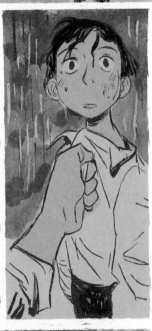

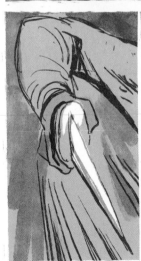

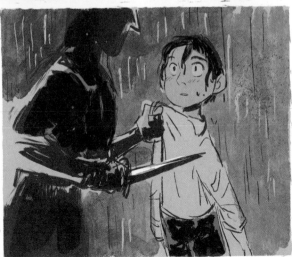

We must guard this secret. It is our duty.
SPLASH!
KICK!
GLUG
GLUG

BWOOOOOM...
FOOSH
HSSSSSSSS
HSSSSSSSS!
HSSSS.
FOOSH
HSSSSS.

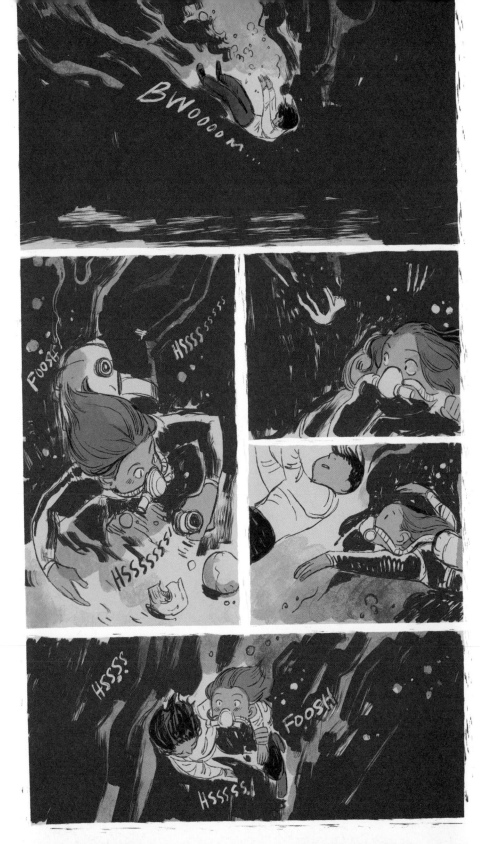

SPLOOSHHHH
ST. LYSE
ORPHANAGE
PLIP
PLIP
PLIP
PLIP
=CREAK=
Dee, what did you drag up this time?

You'll see, Ever. This place, it's a hard life, but you have everything you need.

We'll look out for each other.

But I need to get home. There's something there that I have to protect—

SLAMM
Hello, young miss.
Did this orphanage procure a young boy about four days ago?
That voice . . .
We've had no new boys for a while.

YOU LIE!

Y-y-you must be talking about the dead boy they found in the river.

Dead?

Yes, dead.

CRASH

GRAB

WIPE

You had better be right.

TAK TAK

Why did you lie for me? He could have really hurt you!

I don't know, it just . . . felt right. Like what you'd do for a friend.

We do this for the good of everyone in our city. So they can be safe.

It's my fault he was here. It's my fault that he came after you.

I have to do the right thing, too.

The City of Edmonda.

So the boy is still alive, is he?

So it seems.

This is a loose end, Cooke.

We are aware. The guild will be taking care of it...

Mr. President.

Hello?

Miss Hannah! What a surprise.

Hello, Madame Alexander. I've brought everyone some cookies, for being so nice to me when we visited.

...

Very well ...

No thank you, miss.

Ah! Miss Hannah! You're back!

Hello. Lisa and Anne, right? I have something for you to say thank you for last time.

Well, isn't that sweet of you.

I thought the boy, Ever . . . I thought he might like one, too.

If we want to give him something, we usually have to pretend we don't see him stealing it. He's too scared to take anything we try to give him directly.
But your best bet is to try when everyone leaves, just as the sun is setting. Sometimes we catch glimpses of him.
Thank you!
Hello, who may I connect you with?
Hi, can you connect me to the worst big sister in the world?

Joe? I told you, you can't call me here! I'm working!

When aren't you working, Lisa? I wouldn't ever hear my dear sister's voice if I didn't call the Switchboard.

Besides, I'm about to head to the front lines and it would be tragic if the last thing you did was call me an empty-headed ninnymuggins.

You ARE an empty-headed ninnymuggins.

Ahh, there's that warm fuzzy feeling I was looking for.

Well, there's more warm fuzzies waiting for you when you come back to us!

...

Alright. Well, I just wanted to hear your voice again before I'm off.
Please be safe, Joe. I love you.
Love you, too. I'll see you on the other side.
On the other side.

SLIP

-CLICK-

KEEP OUT KEEP OUT
KEEP OUT KEEP OUT
KEEP OUT
The dust has been disturbed.
What are you doing here?

Oh! It's you!

Don't touch anything in here.

I brought you a cookie.

...

You should leave.

But—

KEEP OUT KEEP OUT
KEEP OUT
Hey, wait!
KA-HUNK
RUMM
RUMMBLE
RUMMBLE
SPIN

Cool . . .
TAK
TAK
TAK
FWIP
KA CHUNK
SPINN

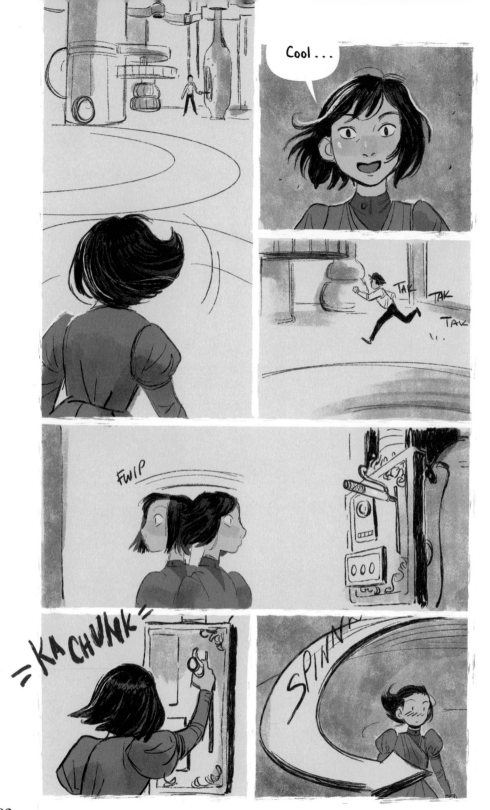

ZWIIIP
WHOOOSH
Drat, I lost him . . .

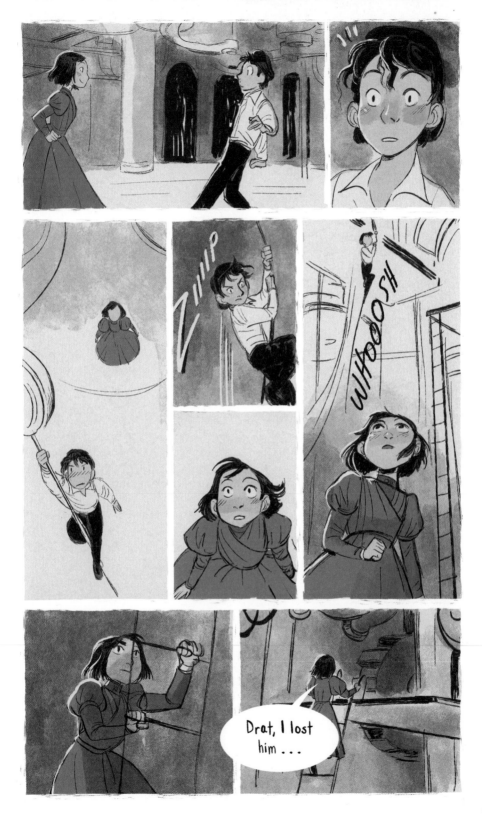

This isn't the place for you.
But I could be your friend. You must be lonely.
I'm not and I don't want a friend.
TUG
SHWING
SWOOSH
SWOOSH

Ever Barnes, if you think you can keep this place all to yourself, you've got another think coming!

TURN
TURN
GLOOWW

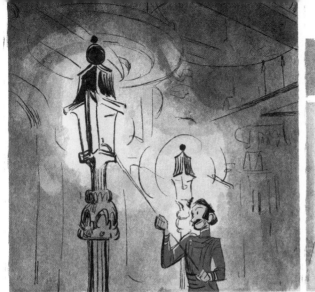

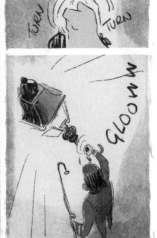

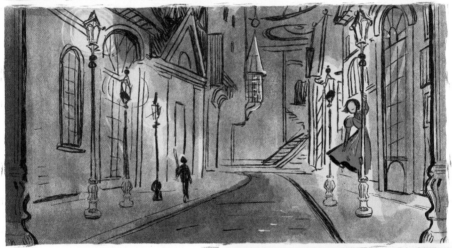

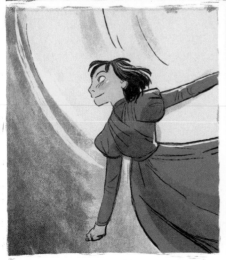

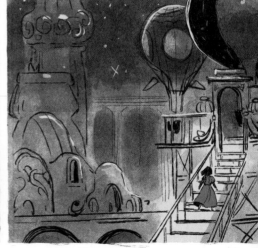

BALLOON STATION
INSTRUCTIONS

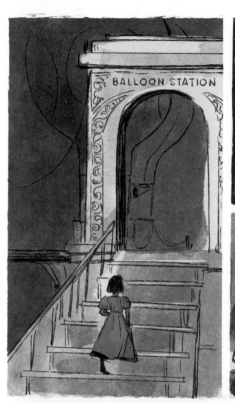

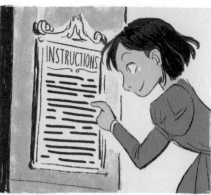

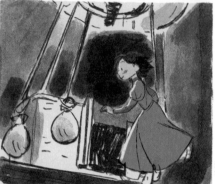

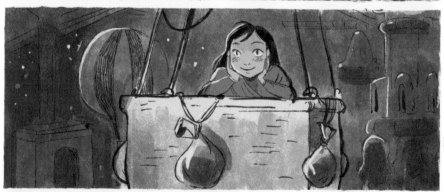

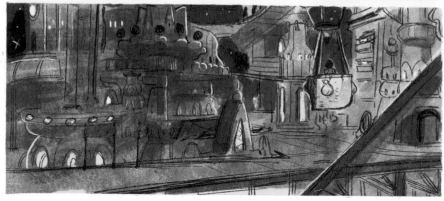

Good thing the servants' entrance isn't locked. Mom would throw a fit.

CLICK
Wheew!
HANNAH!
Mother!

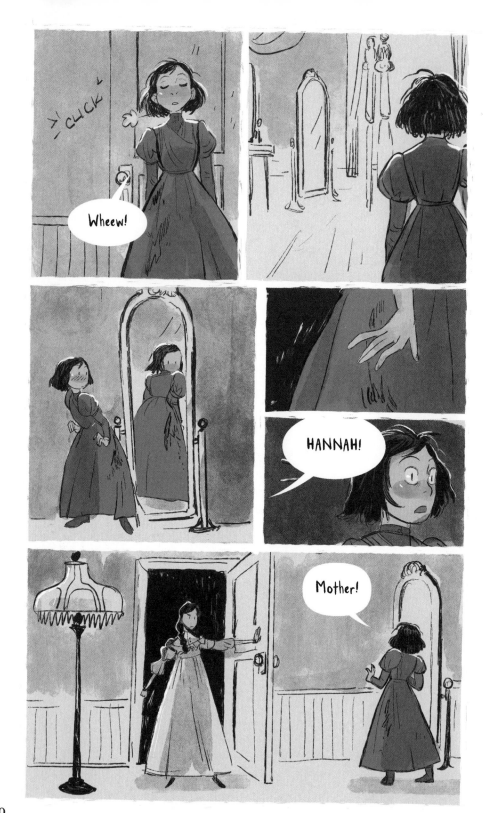

Where have you been? What have you done to your new dress?!

It's nothing. It's just a little dirty!

FLIP

This dress was NEW from the tailor not two days ago!

I didn't want to wear it in the first place!

You never appreciate anything that your father and I do for you!

If you would just let me wear trousers—

TROUSERS? No proper girl would ever wear trousers!

Maybe I'm not a proper girl! Maybe I don't want to be one!

Hannah, you've had more broken bones than all of the boys on Level One combined.

Someday, you will have to grow up and be a real lady. It will be easier if you accept that now.

You don't have much more time to behave like this.

CLOP

CLOP

!

CLOP

CLOP

Is that Lisa?
CLOP
CLOP
CLOP

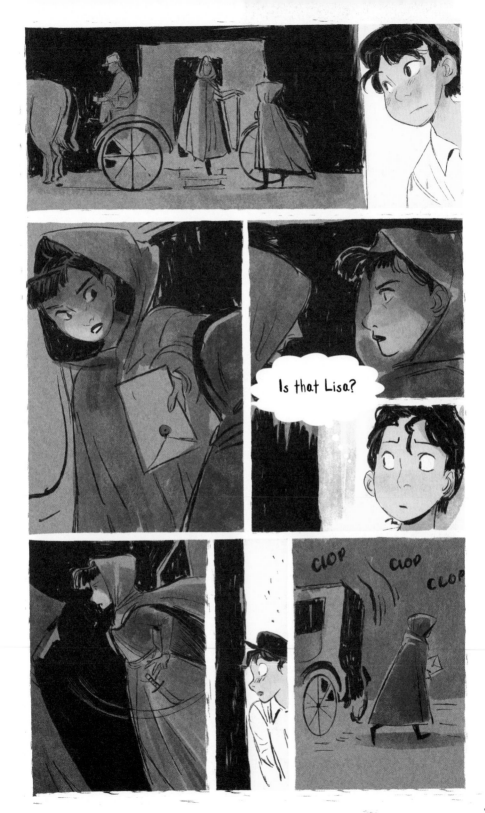

CLOP
CLOP
BAKERY
Oy!

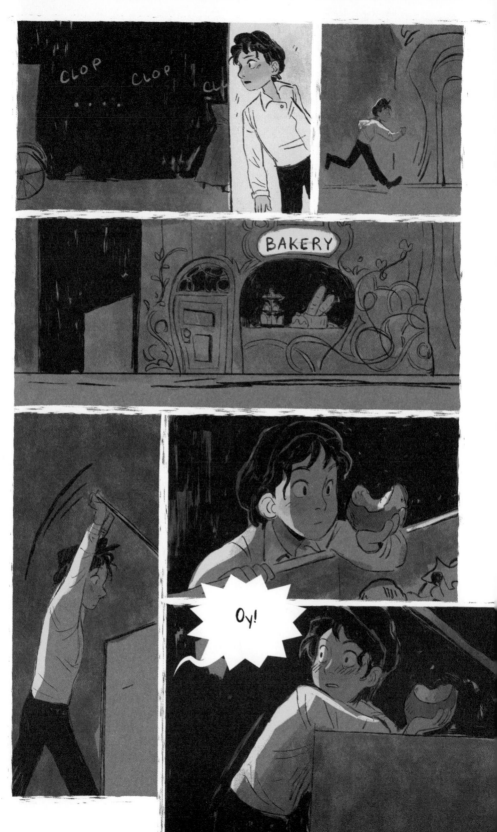

I heard you out here . . .

I won't hurt ya.

WAVE

My wife made too many. They're best when they're fresh.

WHIP

WHIP

Didn't want to make this easy, did you?

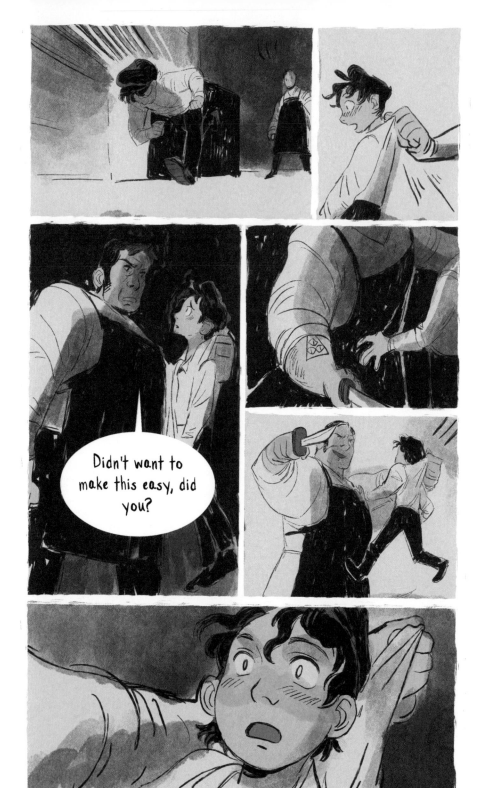

THWAK
SLASH
HUFF
HUFF
HUFF

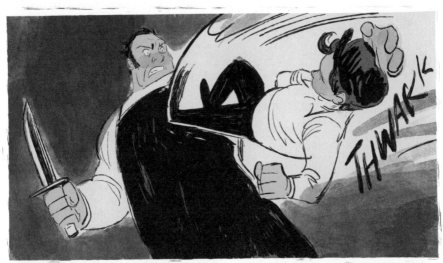

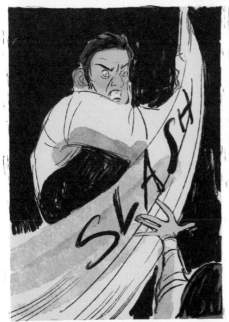

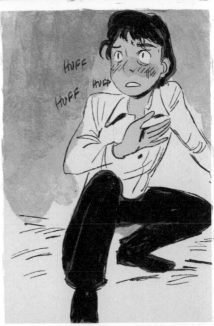

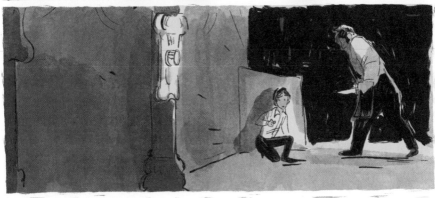

TURN TURN
BWOOOOOM
CLICK

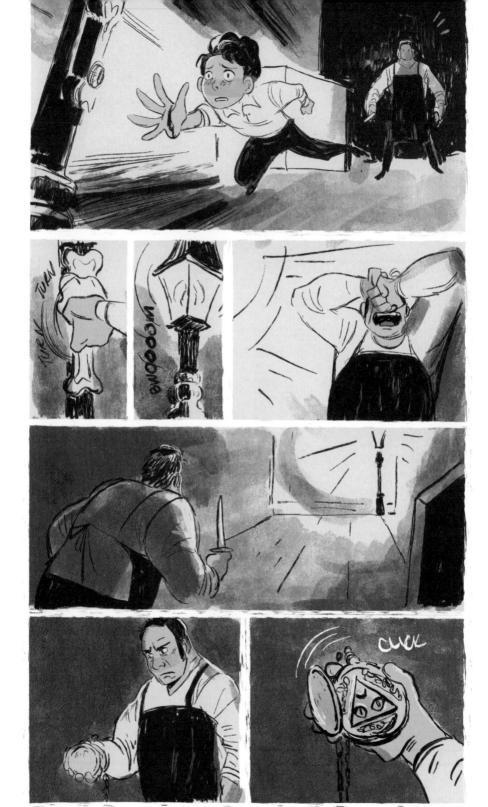

Well?

Well, looks like you and I are in the same boat.

He's a twelve-year-old boy.

And he was only eight when you failed to kill 'im.

He's only still alive 'cause of you.

If it weren't for Cooke, we never would 'ave known that he was in the switchboard building. I would 'ave never gotten a mark against myself. I would still 'ave a clean slate.

I woulda 'ad one less strike against me.

Ain't never known a man with all three eyes on the watch closed that ever saw the light of day again.

Thank ya, Batterbee, but I didn't need the reminder.

So what now? 'Cause of that boy you've got one eye closed and I've got one eye closed.

The only way to open them again is to kill 'im. Strike the fatal blow, open the eye, BAM!

But only one of us gets to do it.

So, it's a race.

War on the horizon with our neighboring city of Edmonda! Read all about it!

Oh! Miss Hannah!

Hello, Lisa!

Looking for someone today?

Something like that.
Well, good luck! I'm sure he could use a friend like you!

FWIP
PAT
PAT
PAT
TUNK
TUNK
TUNK
POP!

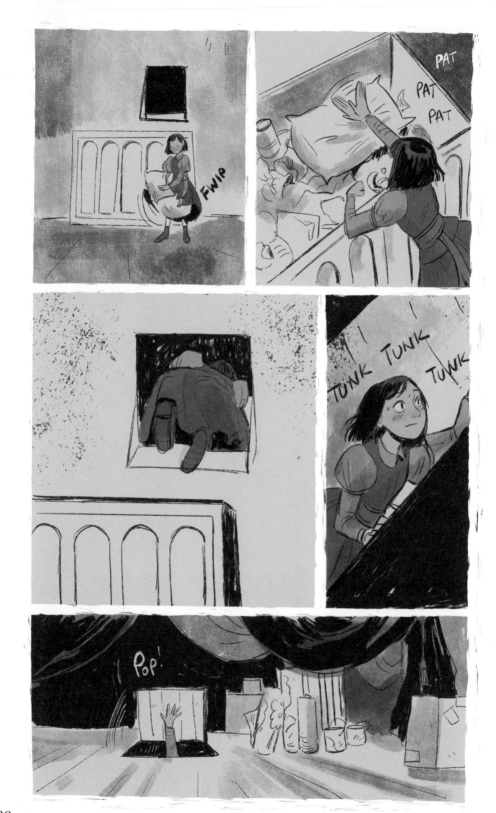

Hello?

I heard you climbing.

I just wanted to see if you needed anything.

I don't.

What happened to—
SPINN
KACHUK
WHRR
WRRHR
SHOOOOP!
WHIP
Just leave me alone!

BEEP
BOOP

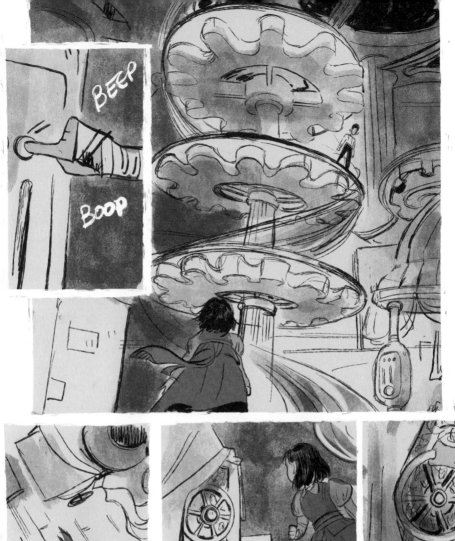

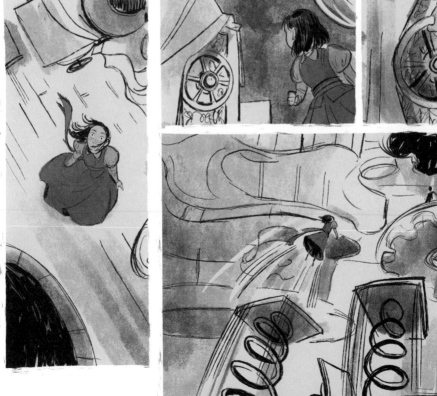

BOOM
How...?
Lucky guess.

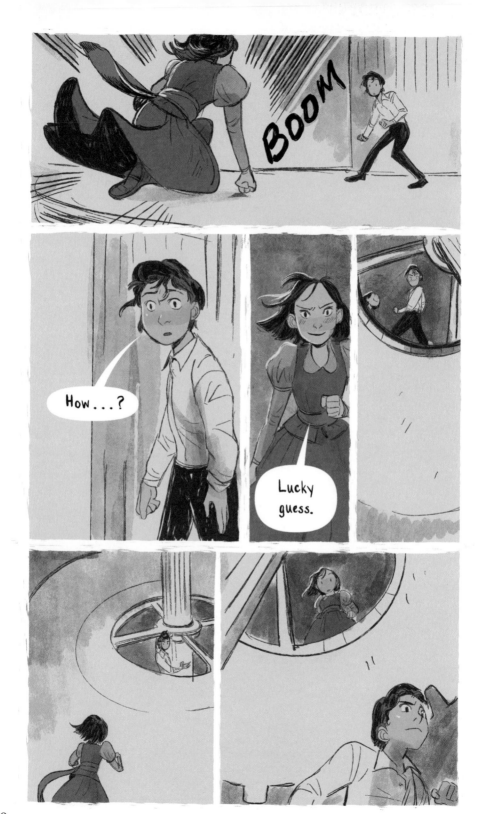

ZWIIPPPP
SWHIPPPP
VRRRRRP

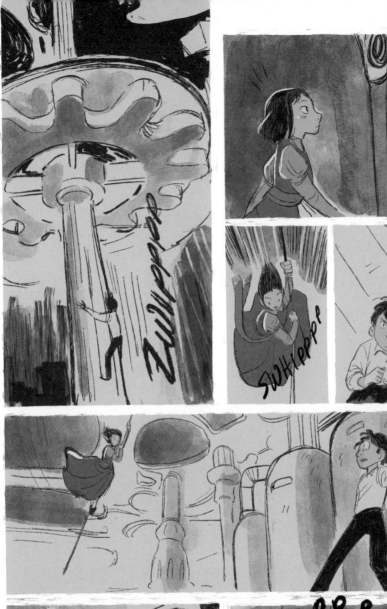

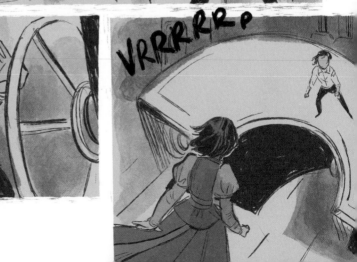

WHOOOOOOOM
HOP
BANG

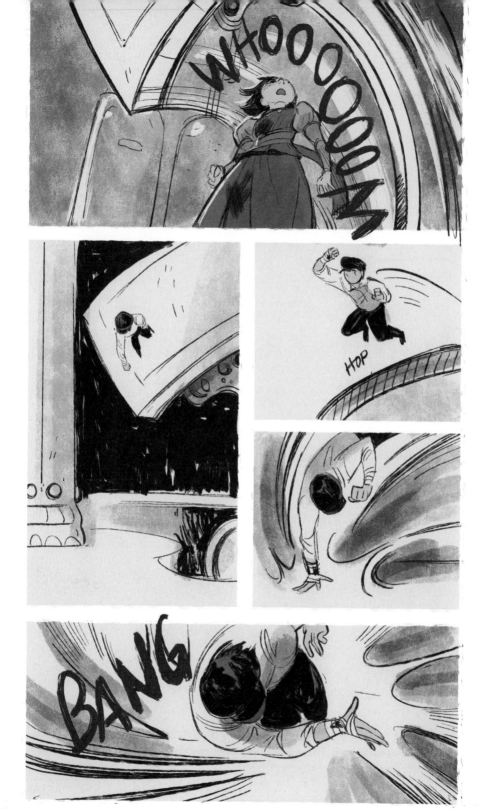

You're hurt!

I'm fine.

Let me help you. I can—

I don't want your help. You think you want to be my friend, but trust me, you really don't. You're just going to get hurt.

Leave me alone! You're just some spoiled rich girl! I'm not just some toy that you can play with. You can't have everything that you want!

...fine. But someday, you might actually need someone's help.

PWOOF

Hannah?

Yes, Papa?
Come and say goodnight to your ol' pa.
SWISH
Well, it looks like someone had an adventure.
Papa, do you remember the boy I told you about, from the switchboard building?

I must find the boy . . . With his father dead . . . and Vash missing . . .

Of course!

I think he's in trouble.

Oh?

But he doesn't want my help.

Glad to be making this deal with you, Mr. Morgan. Happy to see the switchboard building go to such a generous man as yourself.

Pleased to do it. I've had my eye on this place for a long while.

Just so we're above board with everything . . . I should tell you, there are rumors of a young boy living here.

I've heard some rumblings.

We've done our best to cajole him, to get him to an orphanage,

but he's very resistant— and frankly very wily! Nobody has even managed to say a word to him in the past two years.

It's fine. I think I may have a solution . . . You can't force people to do or want things, even children.

You can't force people to do or want things, Hannah.

I guess...

The best you can do is be there for him, be ready... if he does come 'round.

YAAAAWWNN

I'm having such trouble sleeping tonight. Why don't you sing me that lullaby I taught you when you were a baby?

Do you hear the blue jay call, Beyond the bright blue sea? If you can't hear the blue jay call Then we shall never be.

I follow the blue jay's call, Through night I find my way. When you hear the blue jay call, You'll find me there someday.

Ah!
Ever! There's someone I would like you to meet.
GLOMP
This is Vash, an old friend.
Don't be afraid! Vash is a good man, someone I trust.

Would you like some candy, Ever?

Ever! Don't be shy. We can trust him.

Almost . . .
there . . .
HOSPITAL
HOS

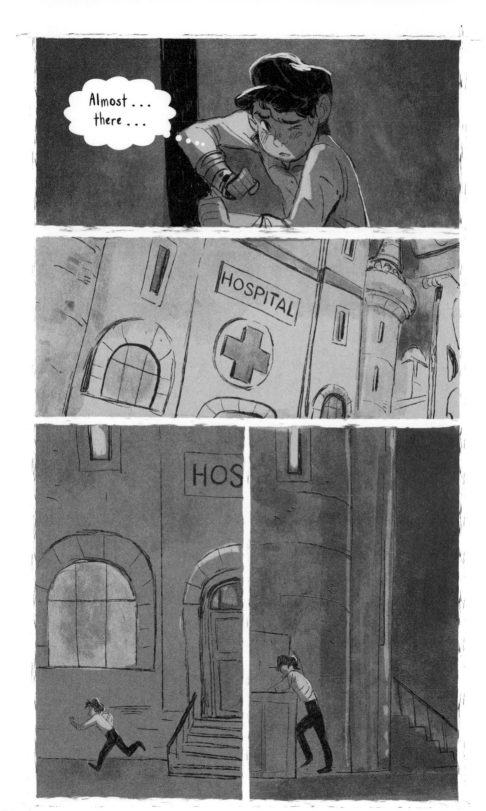

I need to find some medicine. ...
GRAB
SHWIP
It's been a while, boy. Don't cha jus' love a reunion?

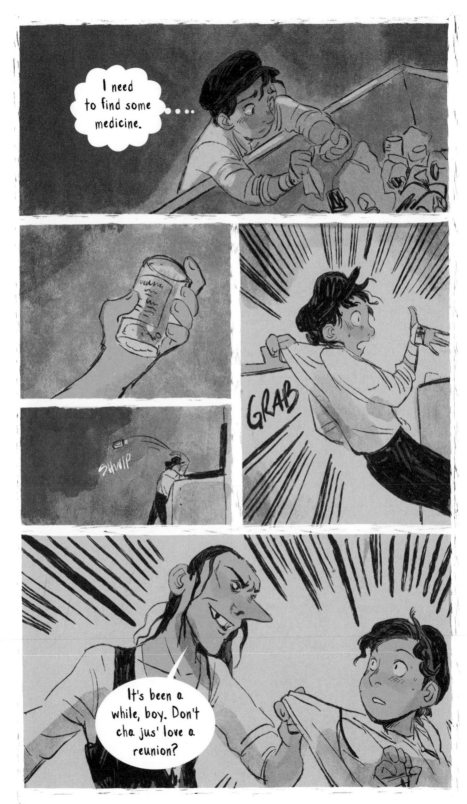

Me? Didn't manage to leave an impression, eh? I thought you 'ad drowned when I threw you into the river, but sadly, no such luck. For either of us.
Who are you?
KRACK KKK
!

You've cost me an eye, boy, and I got to open it!

I'm... too weak to fight back...

It's kind of poetic really . . .
fweee fweeee fweeee
The police whistle! I can't afford to get caught—
fweeee THUNK fweee fwee
fweeee fweee fweeeee fweee

Ever?
Wha-what happened?
Are people often trying to kill you?

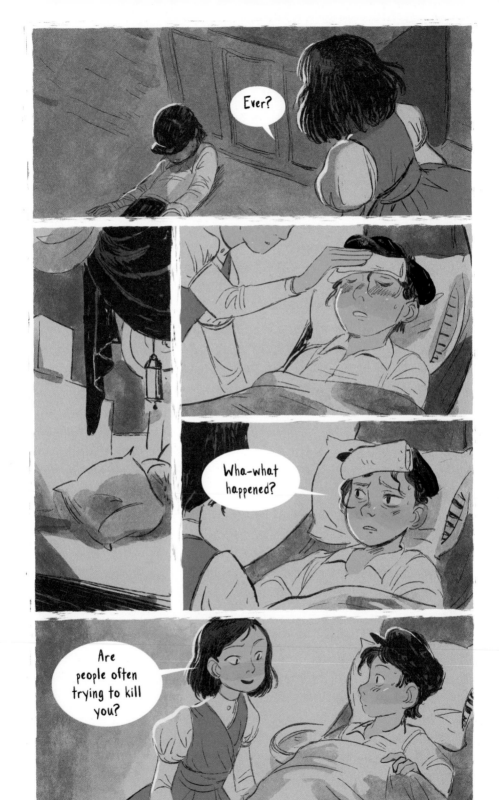

More often than I'd like. What were you doing out there?
I followed you.
Why?
WAVE
WAVE
Ow!
I wouldn't move it for a while. I applied antibiotic cream to get that nasty infection out.

How do you know how to do this?

I used to get into a lot of scrapes, falling out of trees and such. I learned how to patch myself up so my parents wouldn't find out.

I've never climbed a tree.

We should try it sometime.

This one is a favorite of mine. It's about a boy who becomes a pirate. I wish the story was about a girl pirate, though.

I wonder if those men who were after me are pirates. They sure look like them.

I'm not sure pirates like this are real.

They seemed real enough to me.

Yes sir, I'll connect you right away.

Hey, who is that man Lisa's talking to?
I don't know.

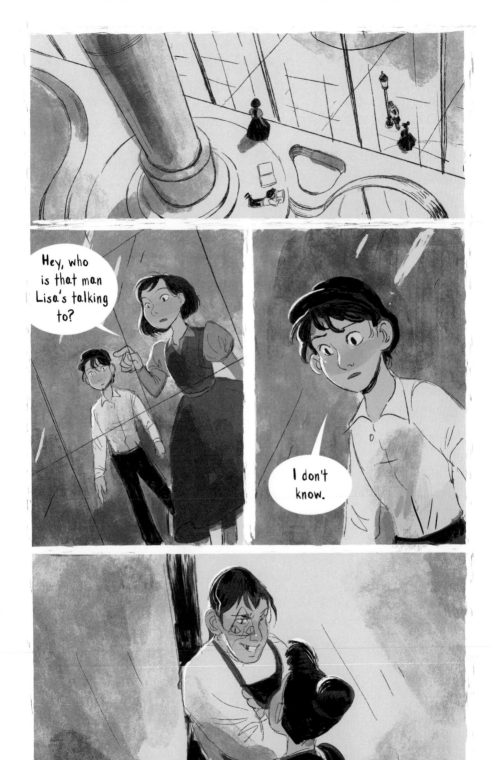

What?
That man . . . his tattoo looks so familiar . . .
No!
The two men who attacked me had the same symbol!
W-w-why is Lisa talking to him?

...
They know you're in here.
Hannah, I need to tell you something about Lisa.
I've noticed her doing things the other girls don't do.
FWIP
I saw her with a knife once.

Lisa might be one of them.

No . . .

She might be after you. She knows you're here.

What can we do?

Lisa doesn't know that we know. We still have the advantage.

The next day . . .

Oh, Miss Hannah!

Hello, Lisa! I came by because I wanted to talk to you, about Ever.

Can you come with me?

Alright.

119

What is it, miss?
You can just call me Hannah.
What the—? Ever?
SWIPP!

What are you two doing? What kind of joke is this?
This is no joke.
Good, because I'm not laughing.
Who is the man you spoke to yesterday? Who attacked me?

What?
We saw you.
And I've seen you sneaking around on Level Three at night. I saw you hand envelopes to a strange man.
...
Who are you? Why do you want Ever dead?

SCHTICCCCKKKk

FLIP

Let's go inside and I'll tell you everything that I can.

123

You were right. I have been hiding something,

but I'm not trying to hurt you. I'm not with those tattooed men.

Who are they?

They belong to an assassins guild. They are known as the Bronze Knife Syndicate.

Then what are you?

... I'm a spy.

I'm a spy for our city. I'm a spy for the Oskarian government.

Why are you spying at the switchboard building?

We hear everything in the facility. I'm assigned to listen in on any suspicious communication between Edmondans and our citizens. I listen for rumblings of movement from their side. I share the information I get with other spies in our network.

Why?
Well, children, you must have heard about the coup in Edmonda. It was violent and quick. We have intelligence that says the new president there will target Oskars next.
I don't know why the Bronze Knife Syndicate wants you dead, Ever. But if you've crossed someone who then hired those assassins, then you two are going to need all the help you can get.
You want to HELP us?

If you leave anything out, I can't do anything for you.

You know my secret now. You have no reason not to trust me. You've already got a guild of assassins on your tail and I might be your only way out.

Okay. I'll tell you what I can.

I see. So these men who are after you must be after whatever is inside of the safe.

Yes, they killed my father four years ago and didn't know that I was still alive. I don't know how they found out.

Okay . . . it's good you told me, Ever. A lot is at stake.

But right now, we've got to deal with these men.

I'll speak to my contacts about them, but I want you two to lie low, keep quiet, and stay hidden. We'll talk again tomorrow and I'll have a better plan by then.

You'll be okay, Ever. You've got me and Hannah on your side now.

Yeah.

Are you alright, Lisa? You look like you haven't slept in days!

Oh, no, I'm alright, I just . . .

Is it because they deployed your brother to the front lines? I'm so sorry . . .

Yes, it's been hard. But with any luck, maybe we won't see war.

We're caretakers, Ever. A secret isn't worth anything unless we keep it from the wrong people and tell it to the right people.

How do we know who the right people are?

I hope so, Pa.

You'll know. If you have good intentions in your heart, you will find people who are like you.

I've got some—

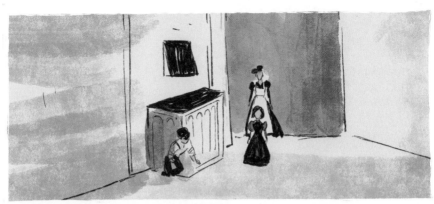

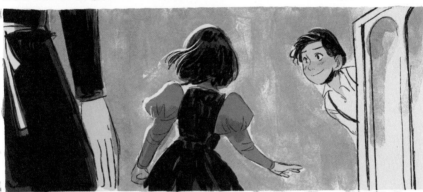

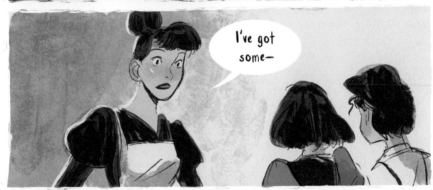

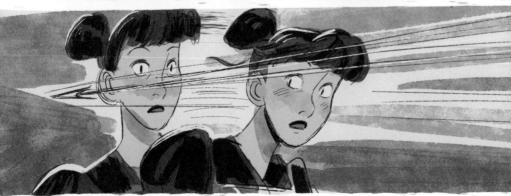

Well...
Quicker than ya look, ain't cha?
Ever, take this.
What is it?

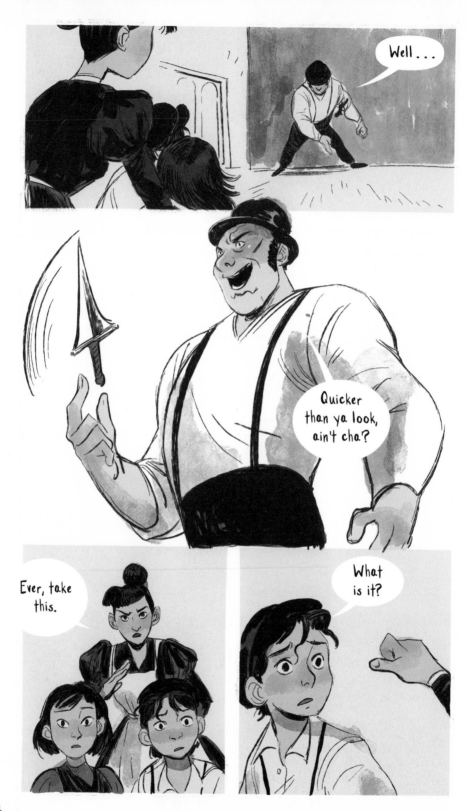

The code, the code to open the safe when you find it.

What?!

There's no time to explain—you have to go now! Get to that safe and open it!

That tattoo... like the one my dad had!

Gwaaaa!

WHOOOOSH!!
BANG
GO!

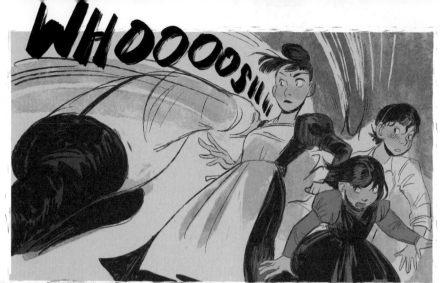

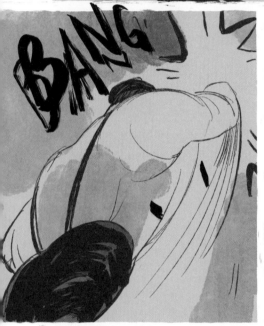

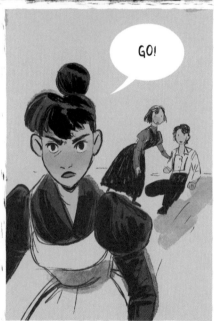

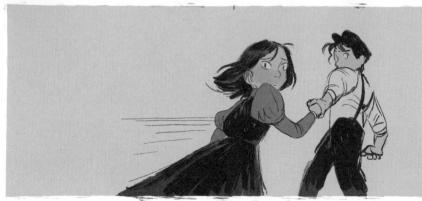

CRUMBLE
I kindly reject your offer of employment.
They said you was a spy, but it looks like you could make a good assassin, too.
SLIP
SHAAAAAA

SHKKKKKKK
SHNKKK
VWIP
ZZWIIPP
He's fast!
AAAAUGHHH!

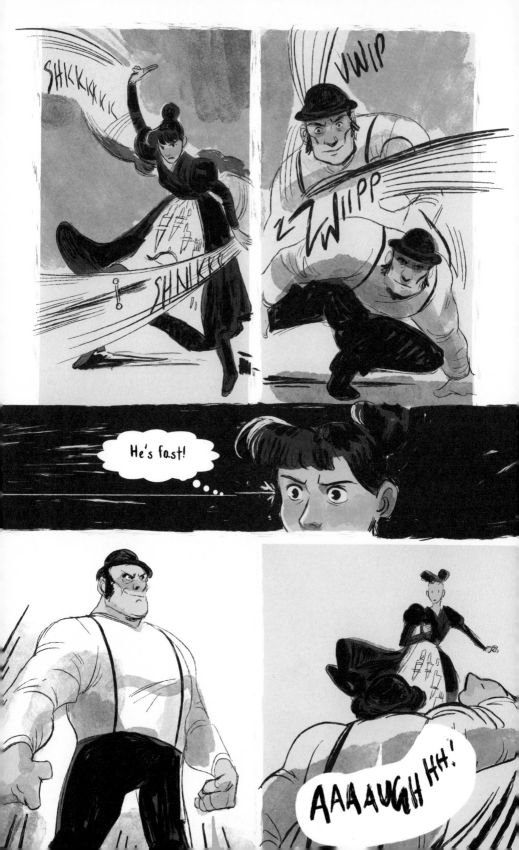

That was the man who slashed my hand. The baker.

What? The baker is a member of the Bronze Knife Syndicate?

NOD

BANG

Now to find the little rat.

You should let me get a stab at him first. He's on my miss list.

That's your business. If I find him he's mine.
Should've expected as much from you, Cooke.
GIVE ME YOUR HAT!
FWIP
FWIP
I'll distract them away from you. You go find and open the safe.

Hannah, they want to kill me! They won't hesitate—
I'm not asking, Ever.
And don't pull any of the levers or mechanisms.
Okay . . . be careful.
You could interfere with the sequence I'll be working to reveal the safe!

TAP
TAP
TAP
BANG!
What are you people doing here?

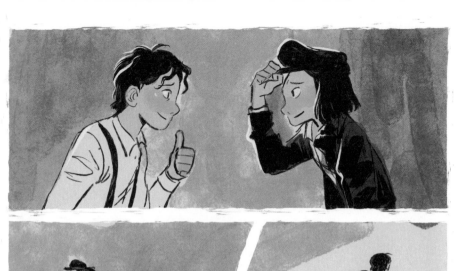

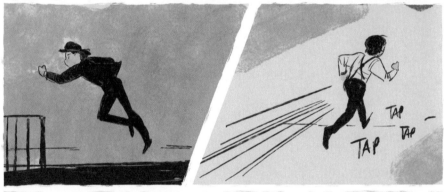

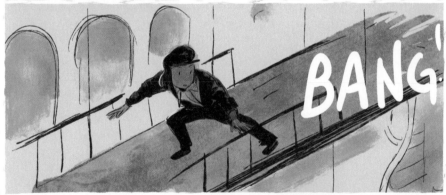

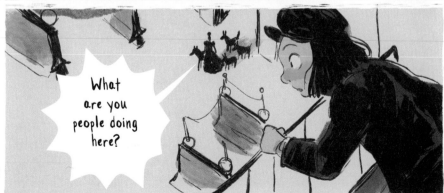

Ah, Madame Alexander . . .

How nice to see you again.

What are scum like you doing in my Switchboard Operating Facility?

Well, we've decided to provide you with a little hands-on service to deal with your pest problem.

That wasn't the deal, Four-Dweller. You don't belong up here.
And I'm the one with the whistle.
ARFF
FWEEEEEEEEE
SNARL
BARK
BARK
FWEEEEEEEEEEEE
SMIRK
SIT
SIT

Ah yes, I did tell you that was the only whistle in existence . . .

. . . but did I mention that its song is modeled after my own special tune?

TURN

GRRRRR GRRRR GRRRR

TWEET! TWEET!

GRRRRR GRRRR

Now, allow us to conduct our business and we will be out of your hair shortly.

BARK BARK
BARK
BARK!
BARK!!
BARK!
There! Up there.
Gotcha.

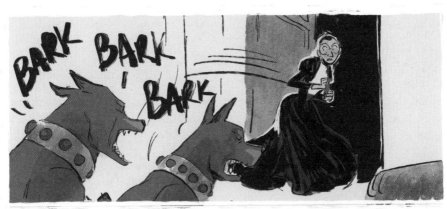

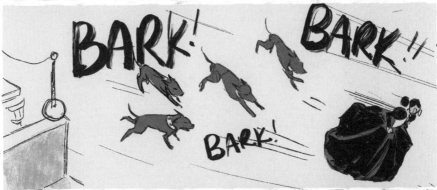

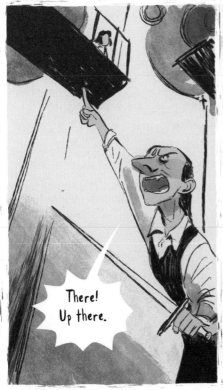

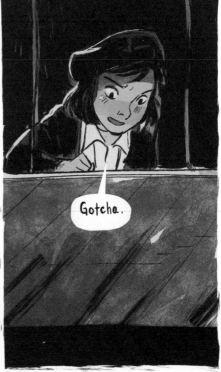

zZIP

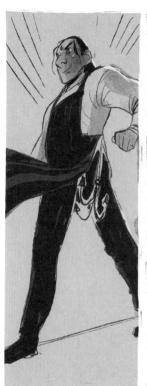

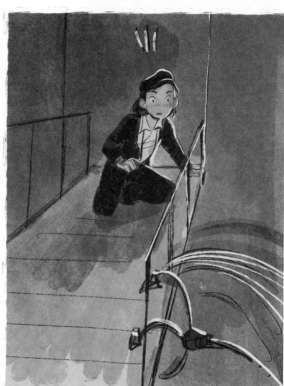

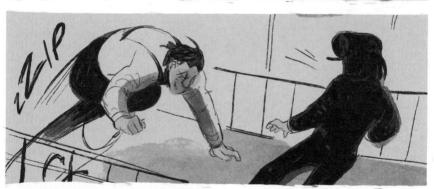

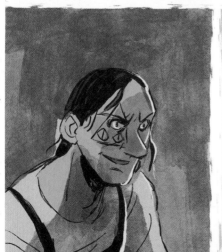

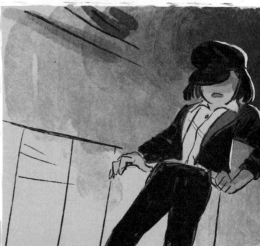

RUMBLE Rumble

SCHWINNG

!

Good work, Ever!

One, two, three to the right, one to the left.

WHIRRR

He's doing it! Vash warned us he would. He's opening the safe!

But how? I didn't see him touch anything.
WHIRRR
HSSSSS
THUNK
HSSSS

Fancy seeing you here.
SKISSIT
FWIP
FWUMP

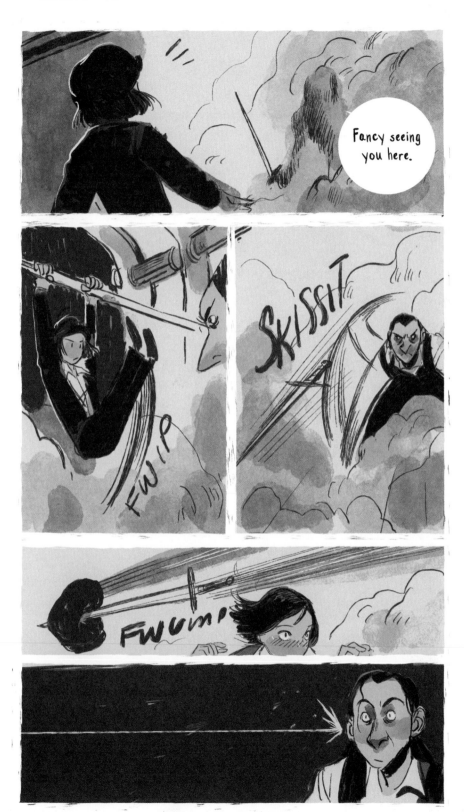

You're not him! You're not the boy!
Drat.
I wouldn't turn your back on me.
KAKR
ACKK
SLASH

SHANK
SNIK
RUMBLE
BOOP
POKE

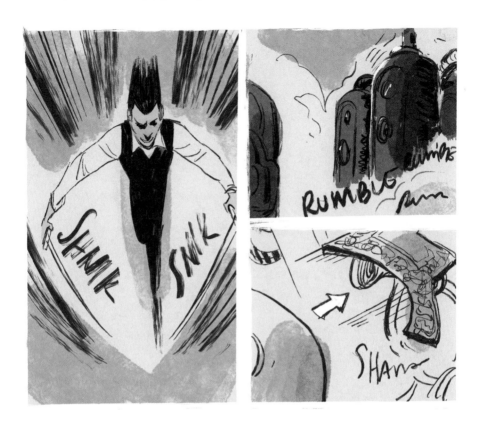

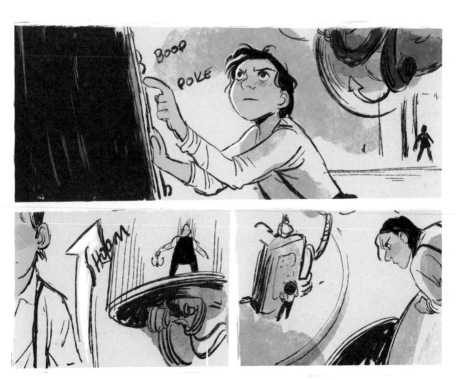

"And don't pull any of the levers or mechanisms."
GRAB
SHAAAAA
FWOOOSHH

There's a pattern . . . Something moves through here.

ARRAAHHH!!!

RRRRR

!!

SLASH
WRRRRRRRRR
!
AAAAHHH

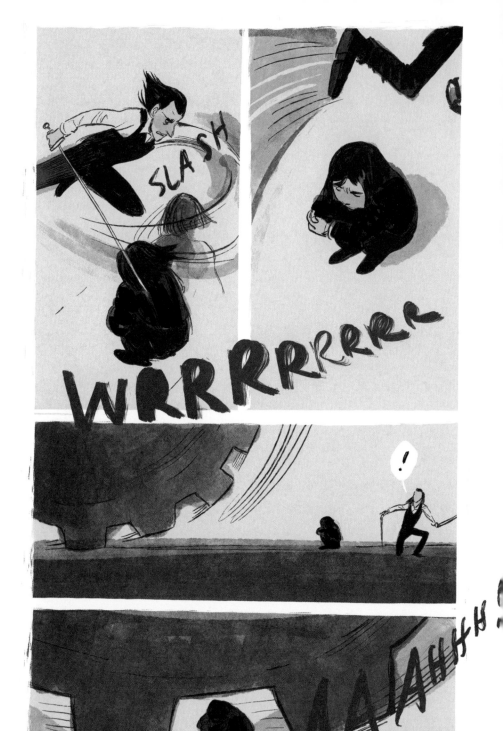

RUMBLE RUMBLE
RUMBLE
TAK TAK
TAK
TAK

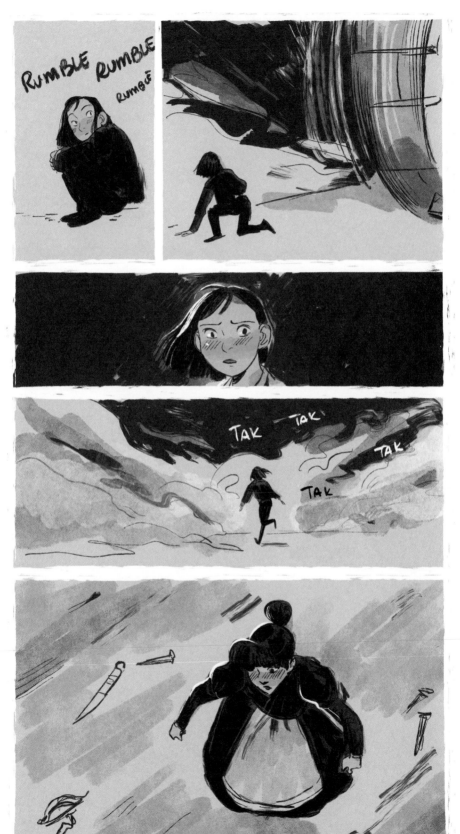

I'll say, it's been a while since I danced with a lass, but it's high time we end this.

I'm out of weapons!

Aww, are ye looking pretty for me, lass?

GRAAA!

WHOOOSHHH

AAAAAAHHH!

WHDOOCH

KRACK

THUNK!

PLINK
PLIP
PLIP
HSSSSS
CHUNKA
CHUNKA
CLICK
CLICK
CLICK
SHAAAAA

I have to give it to you, lad . . .
!
You gave us quite a run for our money. Literally.
KA CRAKK!

AAAARRGH!

SLASH
MISS!
SHWISH
Why you–!
BANG

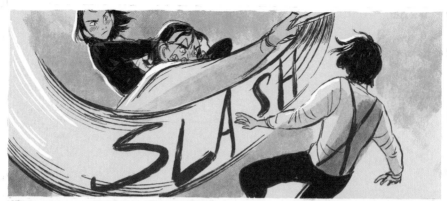

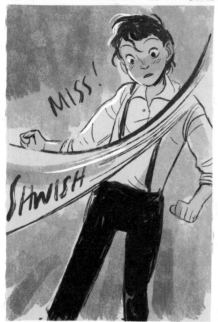

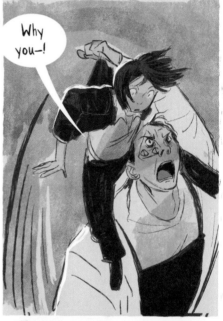

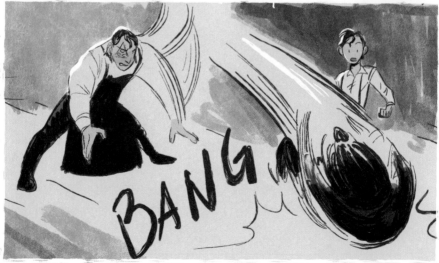

FLING!

AHHHHHHH!
MY EYE!

CKACK!

I've had enough of you brats!
THWAK!!
SLAM!
EVER!!

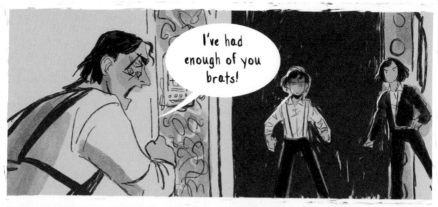

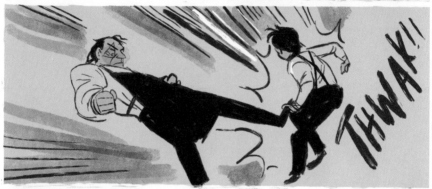

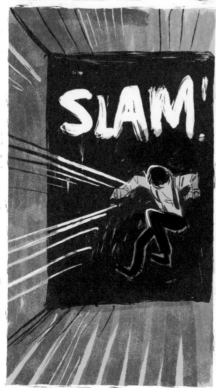

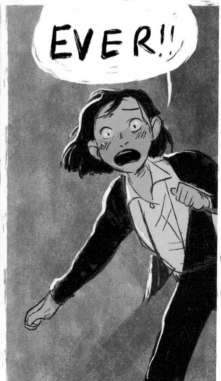

NO!
HSSHHH
HSSS

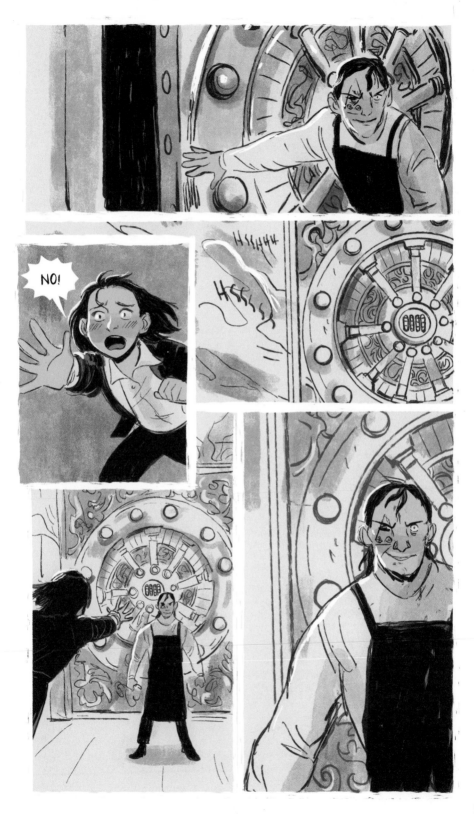

Huff

Huff

Huff

SNIK

At least. . . at least I'll know.

It's . . . empty? There's nothing here.

Ha . . .
Huh
Huff
What was it all for . . . What was it for, Father?
EVER! EVER, CAN YOU HEAR ME?!
BANG
BANG
BANG

H . . . Hannah . . . the code, it's . . . U-J-B-

= PLINK =

= PLINK =

SNATCH

Sorry, little girl, I need him good and dead. He's only got a few more minutes of air left and I can't have you letting him out.

And besides . . . you owe me.

An eye for an eye.

SKIIVV
SLIP
LEAP

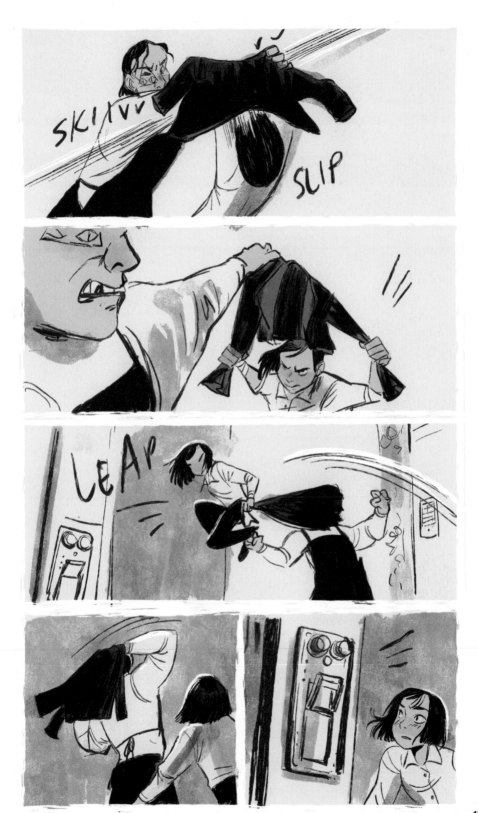

You wretch!

KA CHUNK

Rummm

RUMBLE

SPROIN!

KRASH!

Ever! Ever, please! Tell me the code!

...

Am I too late?

EVER!!!!

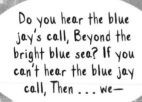

Ever, I don't know if you can hear me . . .

Do you hear the blue jay's call, Beyond the bright blue sea? If you can't hear the blue jay call, Then . . . we—

THRUMM mm
THRUMM

THUMM
THUMM
THUMM
THUMM
Wait . . . we shall never be . . .
THUMM
C
A
J
B
J
B
It's . . . it's a code.
PUNK
PUNK
Hssssss

EVER!!!!
WHUMP

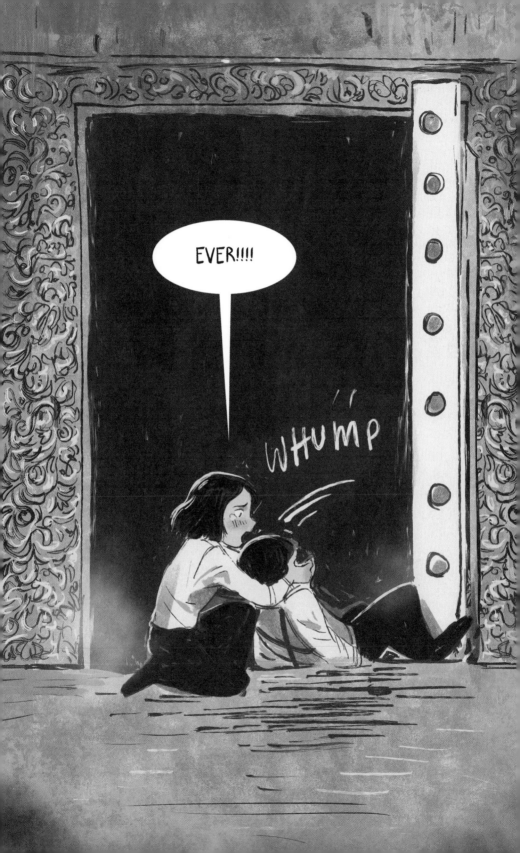

Edmonda

Um, Mr. President.

There's been a development.

The Switchboard Operating Facility in Oskars . . . The caller said that "It's being opened." He said you would know what that meant.

We received a phone call from Oskars.

CLINK CLINK CLINK

CLINK

Thank you, Mary.

CLICK

SMASH!

They can't reveal the Megantic . . . This ends now.

Yes, Commander. I know: Launch the missile strike. Yes.

Now.

What . . . what happened?

That's two you owe me.

It's remarkable. You were seconds away from suffocating, but Hannah got you out just in time.

The safe. I saw it. It's empty.

So, all of it, this, my father's murder, all of it was for nothing. Nothing at all.

Ever . . .

Ever, that's just the thing. It wasn't empty.

Drat, it's almost morning. The girls will be arriving soon.

Hannah, you show Ever the safe. I'll let them all know that the switchboard is closed for the day.

Hold on, how DID you open the safe?

This is going to sound crazy . . .

My father taught me a song when I was little. I didn't know what else to do, so I sang it to comfort you. Then the buttons on the safe started glowing.

The song was the code! Something big is happening here . . .

. . .

See? There's nothing in here.

Ever . . .

Whoa . . .

The bird . . . it's the same tattoo my dad has on his forearm.

My dad had it, too!

So does Lisa. I saw it when the assassins came.

Maybe it's a sign— a sign of recognition. Whoever bears the tattoo is a member of a secret society or something.

A secret society?
Why not? Maybe they even made this mural. But what does it mean?
There must be a clue in the painting. We must not be seeing the whole picture.
It's a map of the switchboard building.

...

No, wait.

No, I think it's a map of Oskars.

...

OSKARS
It's both!
SWITCHBOARD

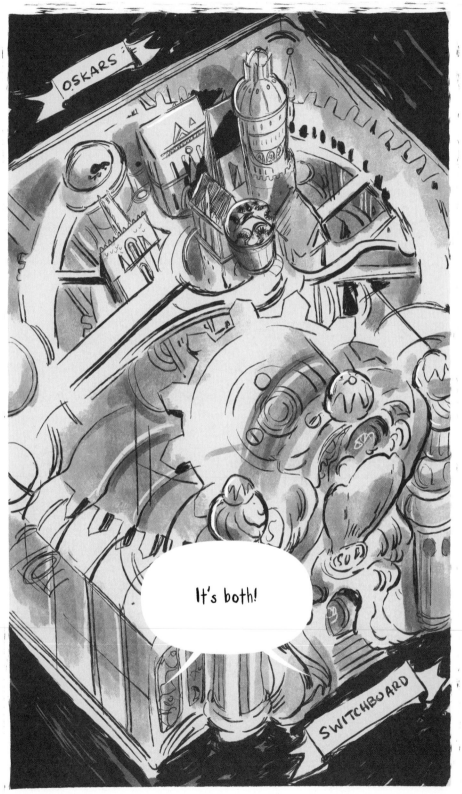

It's like a map. The switchboard building is a map of Oskars!

But why?

Well, if you can manipulate the switchboard building to hide this safe and if the building is really a map of Oskars . . .

. . . then there's another safe in the city — the safe with the REAL secret.

We need to talk to my father.

Your family lives HERE? Why in the world do you want to spend so much time where I live?

I wish Lisa was here!

Me too, but she's got to report back to her superiors and clean up the switchboard building.

Wait here.

Papa?

Ah! My dear, I'm surprised to see you at this time of day! You're usually off adventuring.

Papa, this is important.

Ever?

This is my friend.

Ever Barnes.

Ah, Ever Barnes . . .

My dear boy, you don't know how long I've waited for this moment.

We know about the safe at the switchboard building. And we're in trouble.

What kind of trouble?

With men who want to hurt Ever.

Papa, Lisa told us—

So, you know Lisa as well then?

What else do you know?

The secret, the thing that is going to save Oskars, isn't in the switchboard building.

The building is a map, a model. The real safe is in the city.

. . .

You two have uncovered far too much on your own.

This is a dangerous matter.

You should have come to me, Hannah. But there's sadly no turning back now.

I'm sorry you two have been thrust into this.

You and my father both have the same tattoos. Did you know him?

I did. More than that, I considered your father my friend.

That way, no single family bears the responsibility alone.

If we lost a member, we could still band together to save our city.

Hannah, OUR FAMILY has the secret of the code, taught to you as a song, and also, the knowledge of the switchboard as a model.

The secret of the model was shared with EVER'S FAMILY, who, as I now know, had the secret for revealing the safe in the switchboard building.

LISA'S FAMILY shared the secret of the code with our family. They also carry the fourth secret, which is a mystery to me.

THE DEFECTOR'S FAMILY must have had the knowledge of the sequence for revealing the switchboard safe, and the fourth secret.

One of us did defect years ago. He disappeared and has only recently re-emerged.

He shared your father's knowledge of the sequence for the safe. When he disappeared and your father was found dead,

we believed the defector, like your father, Ever, knew the secret of the switchboard building's movable parts that reveal the safe. When your father was tragically murdered, we then thought this knowledge was lost forever.

Why did Lisa want us to open the safe?

Lisa didn't know that the real safe is in the city itself because that is not her family's secret, but she knew that you needed to work together to defeat the assassins.

So, we were right, the switchboard safe IS a map, showing us how to find the real safe.

Which we must do immediately.

Our enemies know the switchboard safe has been opened. Edmonda's missiles are aimed right at us, to stop us from uncovering any other secrets.

And there's one more thing: Our defector has recently reappeared—as the president of Edmonda!

What does the president want? What's inside the real safe that protects Oskars?

That's not one of our secrets, I don't—

FNUM mop

PAPA!

Well, well . . .

. . . lucky me. I found meself another member of the Canary Society.

I have to get him away from Hannah . . .

You're fast, but you can't outrun my arrows!

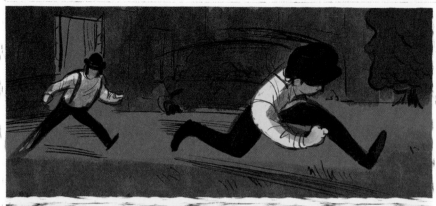

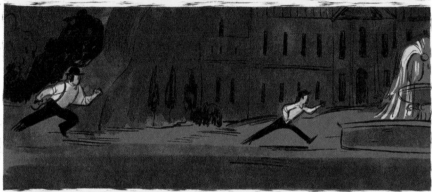

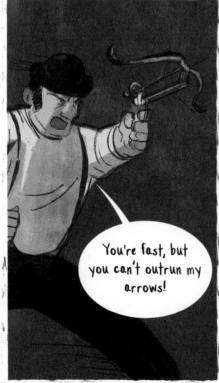

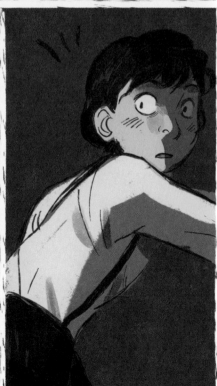

He's right.

What do I do? What CAN I do?

The city, this garden, it's just a giant version of the switchboard building!

What would I do if I were home?

CREAK

Say goodbye.

WHOOSH

BABUM BUMP

!

GROOANN

202

AAAAHHHHH!
AAAAAAAAAA
Goodbye.

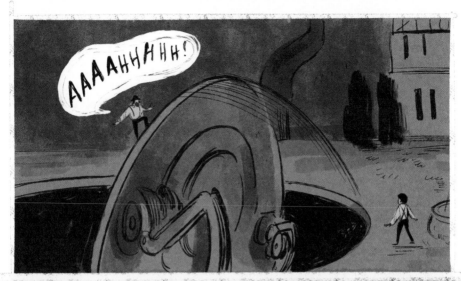

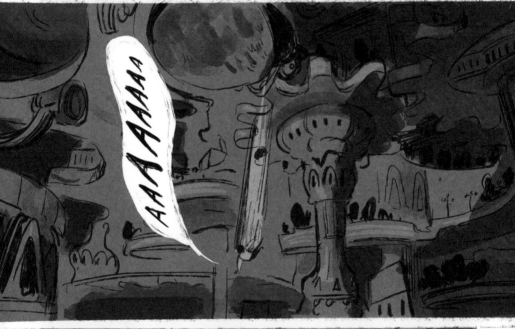

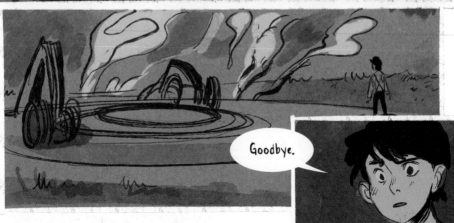

Papa!
Hold on!
Hannah . . .
BROWWOOM
BROW
BROOOOOOM
BROO
BROOM
BROOOM
BRWOOM
BRWOOM

The attack warning! Children, you have to go!

The siren means that Edmonda's missiles have launched!

Vash might guess you are on the trail of the real safe. But it's too late to reach it now. Get yourselves somewhere secure. GO!

Vash...?

No, Papa!!!

I'll be alright, your mother will see to that. Please, my dear. There's little time!

Hannah!

Ever, I can't leave my father! What if . . .

I'm scared, too. And I miss my father.
I'm here with you, Hannah.
I'll always be here with you. I won't let you get lost like I was.
NOD
Everyone to the elevators! We must escape to the lower levels!

We can't run away.
We have to find that other safe and save the city. I can't do it alone. Our task is bigger than both of us. Bigger than our fathers. We're responsible for everybody in Oskars.
NOD
NOD

What do we do?

We have to activate the sequence so we can find and open the real safe.

But how? The city must be ten times the size of the switchboard building.

Bigger, actually.

We'll never make it. It would take all day to reach all of the sequence activation points!

Wait.

The building . . . it's a switchboard building!

What?

It's where every citizen is connected over the phone.

Let's go, we have to get back to the Switchboard! It's our only chance!

Follow me!

The city is just a big version of the switchboard building . . .

Ready?

NOD NOD

SWOOSH

Whoa!
The cart acts like the mail chutes at the switchboard building!
CRASH

Ever! Hannah!

Lisa! The switchboard building, it's a model. The real safe is somewhere in the city! We need your help!

How can I help? Do you need the rest of the Oskarian Central Intelligence?

We need help, but not from them.

We came as soon as we heard. What do you need us to do?

Girls, this is Ever Barnes.

Hello, Ever.

Hi, Anne, thanks for all those apples.

I need you girls to listen carefully. We could stop the missiles and save the city if we work together quickly!

There's a specific sequence of events that needs to happen.

We need to call the houses at these sequence points and get them to perform a task. If we do this right, Oskar will be saved.

Okay, girls, we can do this! Abigail, call number 4312, and hand them over to Ever. Gina, I need you to call 3219.

I've got them!

Hello? Sir, yes, I know the sirens are wailing. But we can save our city. I need you to do something for me. Is there a lever in your backyard?

What? Yes, but it's broken. It doesn't do anything and we can't get rid of it!

I need you to pull that lever down three times and then up once.

And hold on—the floor below you will move!

Let's hope he believed me.

RUMBLE

RUMBLE

HOOOOM
Oh my gosh.
It's working.
KA THUNK
!
BA BOOM

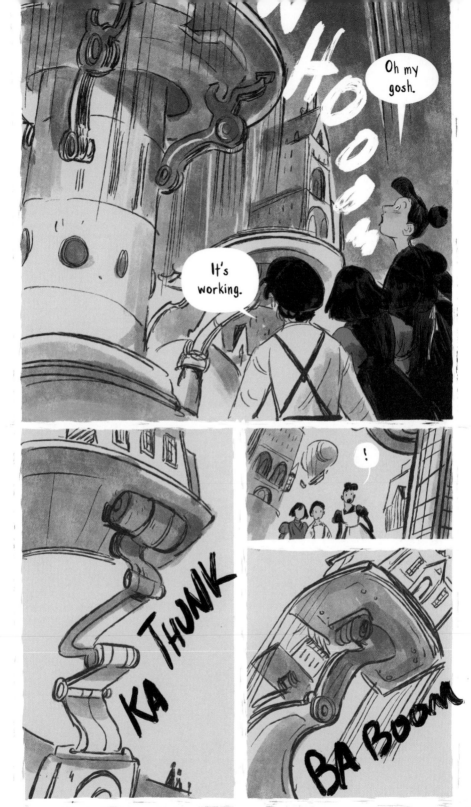

Lisa, I've written down all of the instructions here.
Hannah and I have to get to the real safe!
Got it.
Where's the real safe?
According to the switchboard map, the graveyard.

THOOOOM

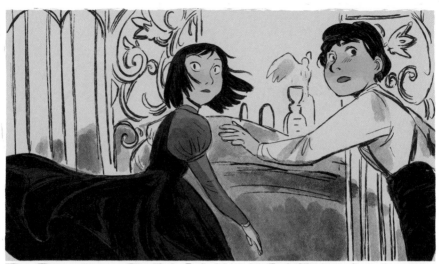

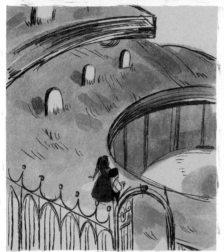

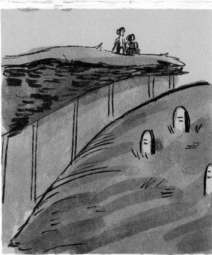

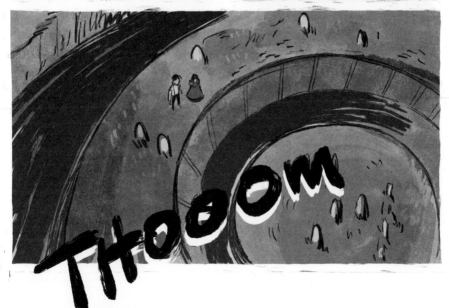

Come on.

SNICK

I wonder how long it's been since anyone has come down here.

I think it's your turn, Hannah . . .
DO YOU HEAR THE BLUEJAY

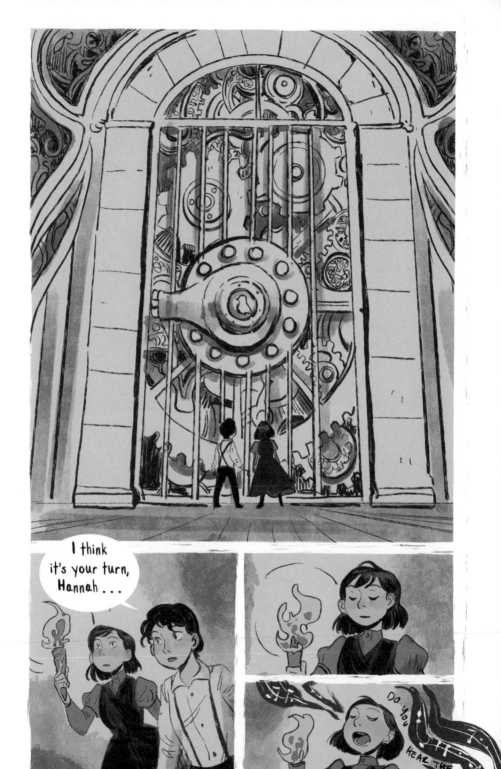

WHRR
WRRRRRRN
HSSSSSSSSS

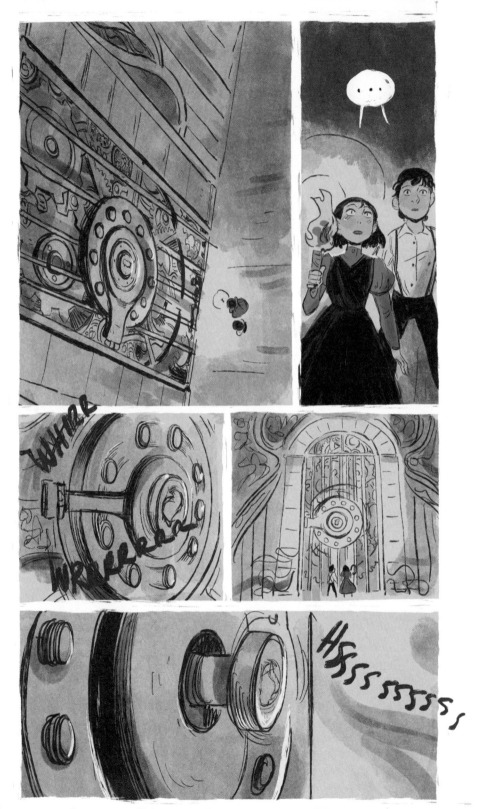

WHOOSH SHHHHH
FWOOOO

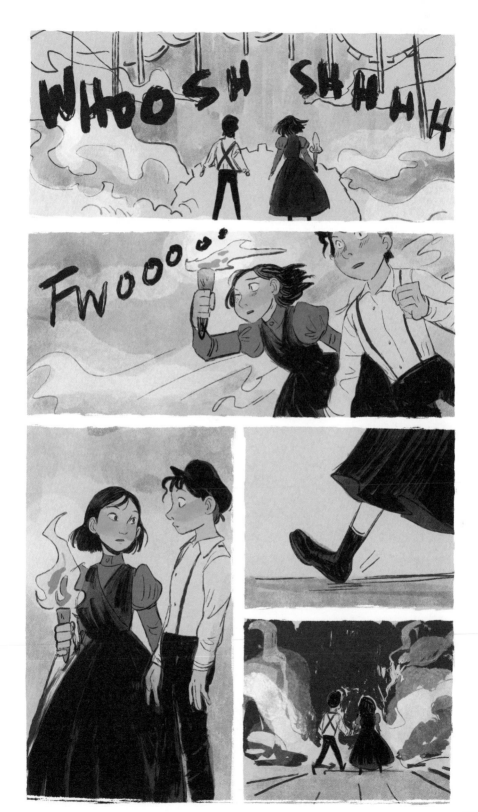

SNICK
SNICK
SNICK
SNICK

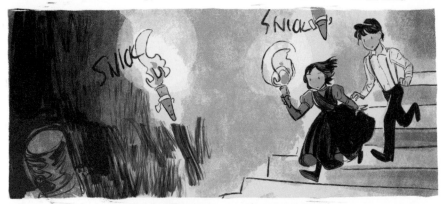

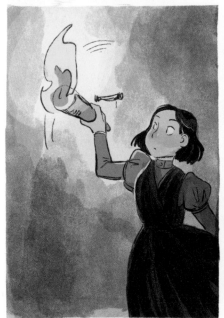

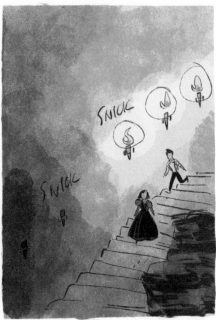

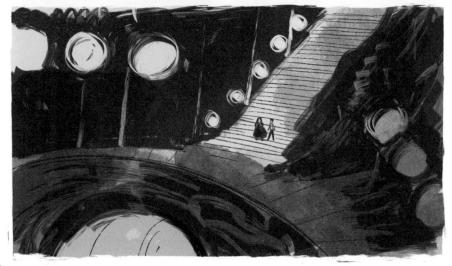

Try your song!
RUMBLE
RUMBLE

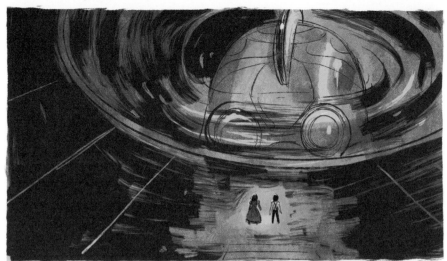

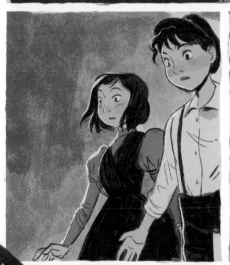

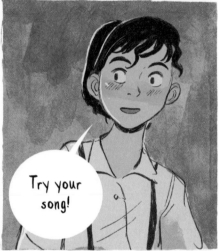

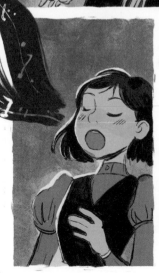

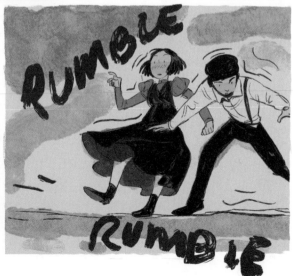

SHOOOOO
SHAAA

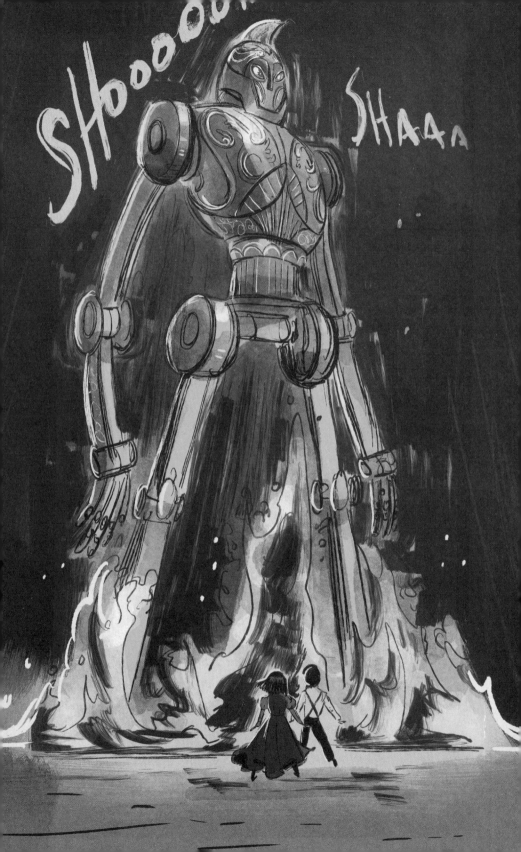

Wh-wh-what is it?
I don't know!

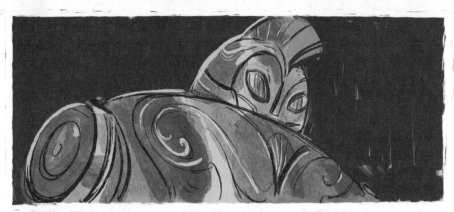

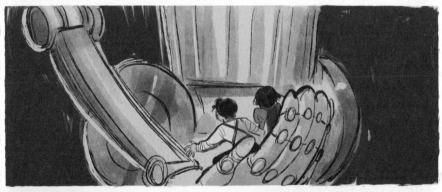

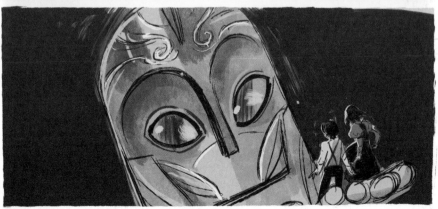

We . . . we need your help!

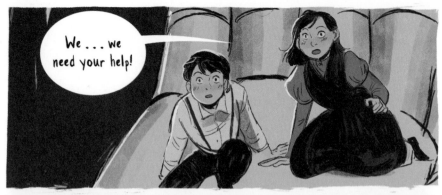

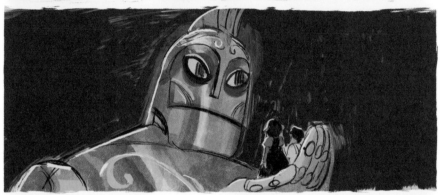

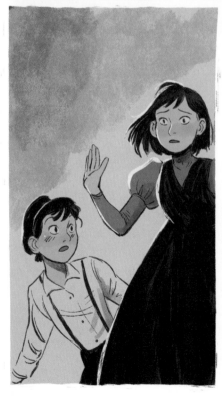

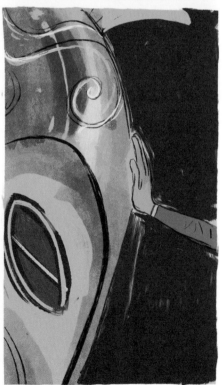

What are we supposed to do?
THRUMM
TRUMMM
Wait . . . these controls.

This is how we pilot it. I think I understand: the pieces that move the platforms are directional like the switchboard building.
I-I-I think I can do this.

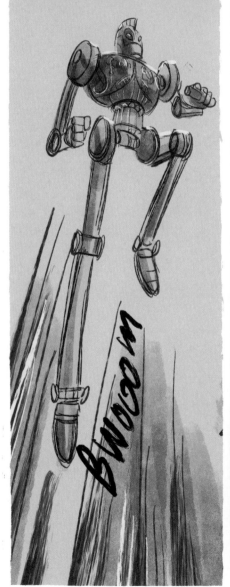

BWOOOM

We're flying!

Ever! The missiles!

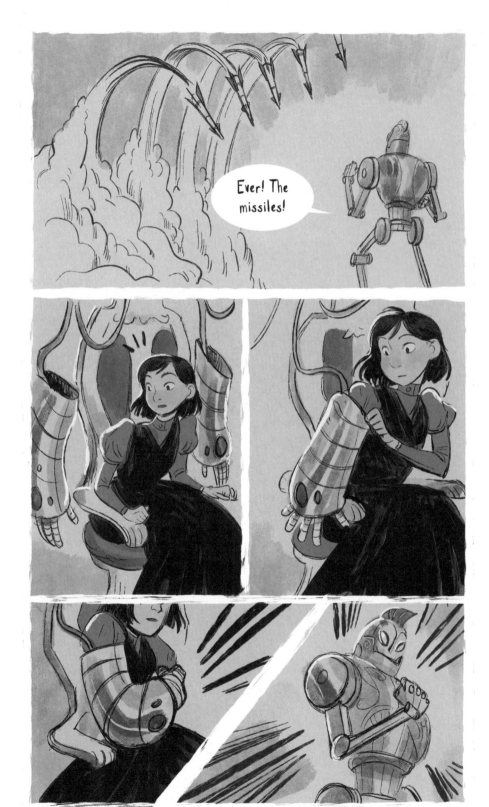

WHOOSH
WHOOSH
Let's punch those missiles out of the sky!
Awesome! I can control the arms!
NOD
KABANG!
BLAMM!

ZAP
Laser zappers?!
Incoming!
ZAP
ZAP
ZAP

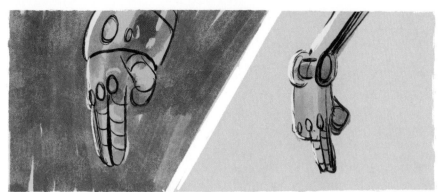

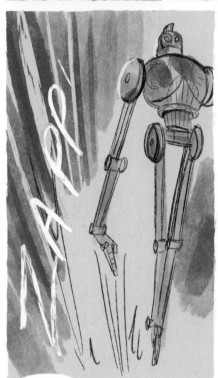

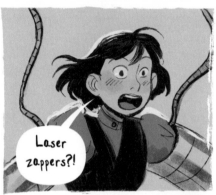

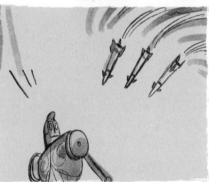

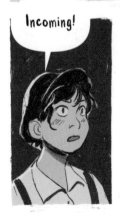

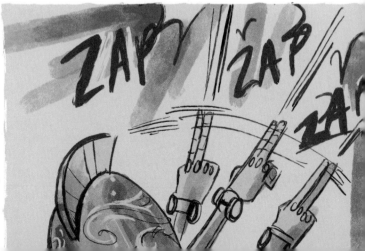

Awesome, Hannah!

Oh no! We missed one!

It's too close to the city for me to shoot it!

VOOOOM
VRRRRRR

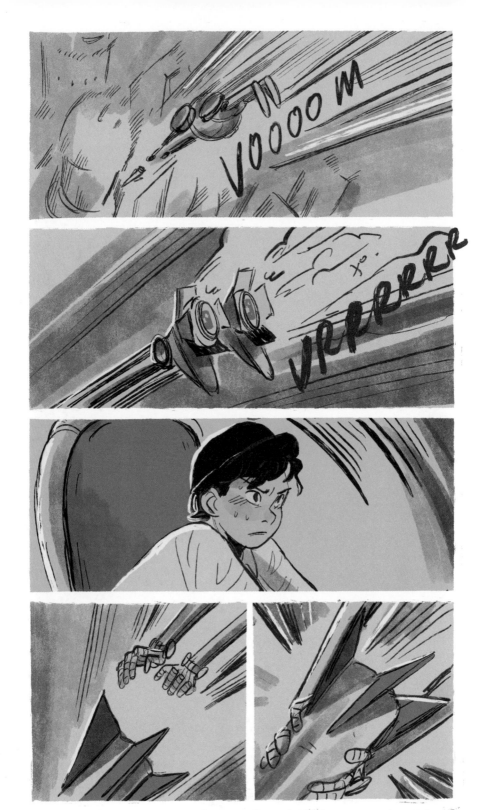

I've got it!
Ever, get us out of here!
FWOOOM
WHOOM
WHOOM
WHOOM
FLING!

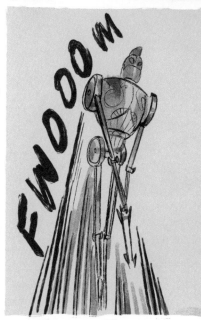

KA SPLOOSH

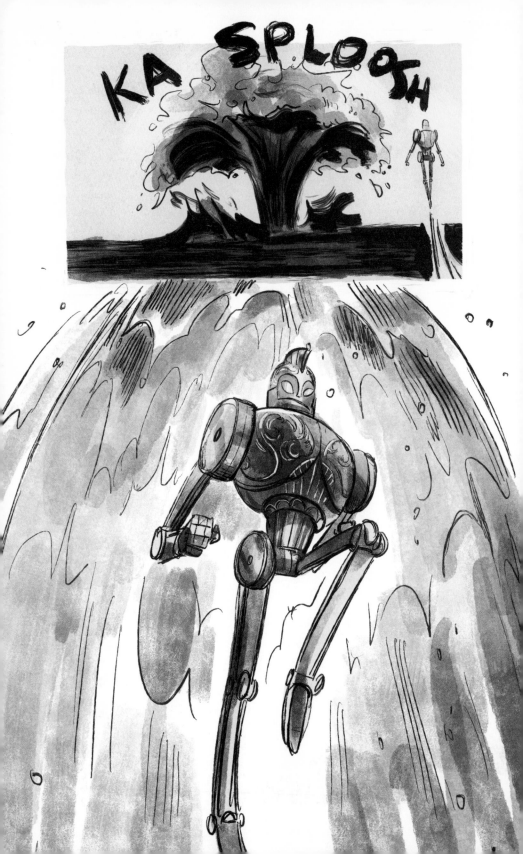

It's alright. I saw.

Um . . . sir—

The first Megantic has been activated . . .

Hannah! Ever! I'm so glad you're both safe!

We flew into the sky!

And we knocked all those missiles away!

I'm glad I was unconscious for most of it then!

Oh, Mama . . .

Hannah . . .

You scared me half to death!

I'm sorry, Mama. I had to.
And thank goodness you did.
And the Megantic! Ever flew it to save us!
Thank you, young man.

Mama, Papa, can Ever come and live with us?

Of course he can! I searched for you, Ever, when your father died. When I couldn't find you, I thought you were gone, too. I wanted to bring you home to us then.

Really?

Of course, Ever. We want you to be part of our family.

Better hurry or you'll never catch me!
Hey! You've had more practice than me!
So, what do you think?

Of trees?

Of everything.

With everyone we met . . .

With all the things we've been through...

Everything is wonderful.

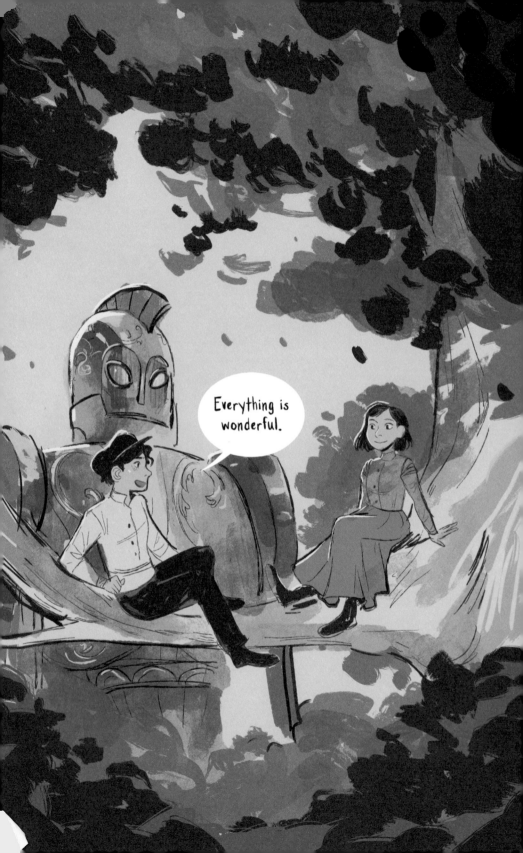

VICTORIA YING is a developmental artist whose clients include Disney Studios and Sony, among others. She has worked on major films such as *Frozen, Tangled, Big Hero 6, Moana,* and *Wreck-It Ralph*. She is also illustrating DC's new middle-grade Wonder Woman graphic novel, *Diana: Princess of the Amazons*. Visit her at victoriaying.com.